MEET TH[...]

Fortune of th[...]

Age: 27

Vital Statistics: Long reddish-blond hair, big blue eyes and the softest heart this side of the Rio Grande.

Claim to Fame: Unlike her driven older brother Callum, Stephanie doesn't measure her success in dollars and cents but in the lives she has touched. The dogs and cats at the Paws and Claws Animal Clinic would agree. So would baby Linus, the child she is fostering.

Romantic Prospects: Stephanie has kissed enough frogs to doubt that her Mr. Right even exists.

"I'm tired of waiting for love to happen. That's why I began proceedings to foster or adopt a child. When Linus came into my life, I finally felt complete. And then I met Acton Donovan.

"It's silly to imagine a sexy rancher like Acton would even be interested in someone serious like me. Besides, the timing is all wrong. He's too young to be thinking about settling down and starting a family. And I'm too smart to repeat my past mistakes. That doesn't seem to matter, though, when Acton aims that gorgeous cowboy smile at me..."

Dear Reader,

Welcome back to Rambling Rose, Texas, where one branch of the Fortune family is already making big changes around town. All in the name of progress, of course! But as far as my heroine, Stephanie Fortune, is concerned, she doesn't care about her brothers' construction plans or their ideas to make Rambling Rose more progressive. All she cares about is her job as a veterinary assistant and being a foster mother to baby Linus.

Having a husband and children of her own is something Stephanie has wanted for years, but after several disappointing attempts at romance, she's given up on finding a man who might genuinely love her. And even though she's presently taking care of Linus, she could lose the baby at any moment if his real parents decide to show up and claim him.

But Valentine's Day is fast approaching, and when a tall, dusty cowboy walks into the clinic with an adorable dog at his side, Stephanie is suddenly seeing the family she's always wanted. But is she capable of lassoing his heart?

I hope you enjoy reading how Stephanie and Acton find true love, and that your Valentine's Day is filled with everything that puts a smile in your heart.

Warmest wishes,

Stella Bagwell

Fortune's Texas Surprise

Stella Bagwell

HARLEQUIN
SPECIAL
EDITION

Special thanks and acknowledgment are given
to Stella Bagwell for her contribution to
The Fortunes of Texas: Rambling Rose miniseries.

ISBN-13: 978-1-335-89434-2

Fortune's Texas Surprise

Copyright © 2020 by Harlequin Books S.A.

This edition published by arrangement with Harlequin Books S.A.

For questions and comments about the quality of this book,
please contact us at CustomerService@Harlequin.com.

Harlequin Enterprises ULC
22 Adelaide St. West, 40th Floor
Toronto, Ontario M5H 4E3, Canada
www.Harlequin.com

Printed in U.S.A.

After writing more than eighty books for Harlequin, **Stella Bagwell** still finds it exciting to create new stories and bring her characters to life. She loves all things Western and has been married to her own real cowboy for forty-four years. Living on the south Texas coast, she also enjoys being outdoors and helping her husband care for the horses, cats and dog that call their small ranch home. The couple has one son, who teaches high school mathematics and is also an athletic director. Stella loves hearing from readers. They can contact her at stellabagwell@gmail.com.

Books by Stella Bagwell

Harlequin Special Edition

Men of the West

Her Kind of Doctor
The Arizona Lawman
Her Man on Three Rivers Ranch
A Ranger for Christmas
His Texas Runaway
Home to Blue Stallion Ranch

The Fortunes of Texas: The Lost Fortunes

Guarding His Fortune

Montana Mavericks: The Lonelyhearts Ranch

The Little Maverick Matchmaker

Montana Mavericks: The Great Family Roundup

The Maverick's Bride-to-Order

Visit the Author Profile page
at Harlequin.com for more titles.

A big thank-you to animal shelters
and the devoted workers who give our
needy furry friends a special home.

Chapter One

A cold north wind swooshed past Stephanie Fortune as she stepped through the glass door of the Rambling Rose Pediatric Center, but the tiny baby bundled in a heavy blue blanket was snug and warm in her arms as she carried him down a short corridor and into the busy day-care center.

As she made her way through a large room filled with shrieks of laughter and squeals from a group of preschool children, a few of the busy staff members glanced in her direction and waved. Stephanie waved back and continued walking until she reached a wide door that led to an area designated for babies under twelve months of age.

After a short knock, the door swung wide and Alaina, a middle-age woman with a kind face, greeted her with a cheery "good morning" and immediately followed it with a disapproving eye on her thin jacket.

"Young lady, how long is it going to take you to remember you're living in Texas now, not Florida? You're going to freeze without a proper coat!"

"I haven't had time to buy any winter clothing. Besides, most of the locals tell me that spring comes early to this part of Texas. And as long as little Linus is warm and comfy that's all I care about."

Stephanie flipped the blanket off the baby's head and smiled lovingly down at the four-week-old boy. According to his pediatrician, Dr. Green, the baby had been born three to four weeks early. But thankfully, his birth weight had been enough to keep him out of neonatal care.

"It wouldn't be good for his mother to come down with a cold," Alaina said. "You might give him the sniffles."

Unfortunately, Stephanie wasn't Linus's real mother. No one in Rambling Rose, or points beyond, seemed to know where Laurel, the biological mother, had gone after she'd walked into the pediatric center and left the infant with a nurse at the front desk. Since then, Stephanie had been the boy's foster mother, and with each passing day she was beginning to regard the baby as her own son.

"I never get a cold," Stephanie assured her, then bent down her head and pressed a kiss to Linus's smooth forehead. He smelled of baby oil, powder and the formula he'd nursed only minutes before she'd made the drive into town. The scents, along with the warm weight of his little body tucked into the crook of her arm, comforted her. "And as long as Linus's mother is missing, I'm going to give him the best care I can."

"I'm sure you get tired of people asking, but have you heard any news about her?" Alaina asked.

Mixed emotions swirled inside Stephanie as she studied Linus's little pug nose, bow-shaped mouth and dark blue eyes, which were not yet developed enough to focus on much more than movements directly in front of his face. Like everyone in Rambling Rose, Stephanie hoped Linus's biological mother was alive and safe. On the other hand, she'd wanted a child of her own for a long, long time, so ever since she'd suddenly been given the chance to be a foster mother to Linus, she'd felt like her life was a dream come true. Yet, each day she had to force herself to remember that Linus didn't actually belong to her. It would be a year or more before she might get the chance to adopt him legally, and before that happened, Laurel might have a change of heart and show up to claim her son.

"No news at all," Stephanie said, answering the woman's question. "Dr. Green believes she could be suffering from postpartum depression or maybe even some sort of psychosis. But she wasn't his patient, so he's only guessing."

"Well, you're doing a wonderful job with Linus," Alaina assured her, then held out her arms for the baby. "And from what I hear you're doing a bang-up job at the Paws and Claws Animal Clinic. Frankly, I don't know how you handle both. Every time I pass the new building, the parking lot is overflowing with vehicles."

Stephanie handed over Linus and a heavy diaper bag to Alaina. "The animal clinic is very busy," she agreed. "And today is spay-and-neuter day, so we'll be even busier than usual." She glanced at a large clock hanging on the wall. "Which means I'd better be going."

Stephanie gave Linus a goodbye kiss, then hurried out of the day care. As she drove to Paws and Claws Animal Clinic, she thought about the millions of other mothers who had to leave their children at day care while they worked at a job they either loved or simply endured to help pay the bills at home.

Thankfully, Stephanie loved her job as a veterinary assistant and she didn't have to worry about making her paycheck stretch to cover essentials. She realized there were some folks around Rambling Rose who assumed she'd inherited her wealth because her last name was Fortune. But that wasn't entirely the case. She'd worked hard to acquire her college education and later support herself in her chosen profession.

In less than five minutes, Stephanie arrived at Rambling Rose's animal clinic and rescue facility. The new sprawling building that housed Paws and Claws had been built by her three brothers, who owned and operated Fortune Brothers Construction. The modern structure of white brick and brown trim was a far cry from the cramped space of the old clinic that had served the community for many years. So far, Dr. Neil and the whole staff were enjoying the updated treatment rooms and a waiting area large enough to accommodate the daily influx of patients.

Stephanie entered the building through a back entrance and went straight to a small break room to stow her jacket and handbag in a locker. As she turned the dial of the combination lock, an excited female voice sounded directly behind her right shoulder.

"Stephanie! Oh, wow, are you going to be extra glad you came to work early this morning!"

Stephanie turned away from the block of metal lockers to see Monica, a young woman who worked in the clinic's bookkeeping department. From the animated look on her face, something unusual was going on.

Combing fingers through her long, windblown red hair, Stephanie said, "I'm always extra glad to be at work, Monica. What's so different about today?"

"Because he's in the waiting room! With his dog! It been ages since he's been in the clinic and now—finally—he's back!"

Stephanie refrained from rolling her eyes as she pinned a name tag to the thin black sweater she was wearing with her blue jeans. At twenty-seven, she'd had far too many dating disappointments to let herself get excited over a man.

"He?" she asked with casual indifference. "Who is this man that's got you all gaga this morning?"

"Acton Donovan! His family owns a ranch not far from town. And believe me, Stephanie, there's no other man in Rambling Rose like him! He's cute and sexy and adorable and—"

"Whoa!" Stephanie held up a hand. The only kind of guys Stephanie had been able to find were those who'd been more concerned about their own personal wants and needs, but Monica didn't need to know that. "There's no such man that you're describing. He'd be too good to be true. And I have work to do."

She started out of the break room with Monica stalking her heels. "All right, you don't have to believe me," she said under her breath. "You'll see for yourself when Dayna brings him and his dog back to an examining room. So be prepared. That's all I can say!"

Stephanie cast her an indulgent smile. "Don't worry, Monica, I won't faint at the sight of Mr. Hunky."

"Stephanie, when it comes to men, it's like you're from another planet!" With an exasperated grunt, Monica hurried on past Stephanie and disappeared through a door to the accounting office.

Stephanie walked on toward the examining rooms, then stopped in midstride as she saw the door to the waiting room open and Dayna usher in the next patient, which, in this case, was a long-haired dog that appeared to be a mix of cocker spaniel and Australian shepherd. She was thinking how adorably cute the dog was when the owner suddenly appeared through the door, and for one ridiculous second her breath caught in her throat.

This had to be the dream man Monica had been raving about. Dressed in faded denim, dirty cowboy boots and a chocolate-brown Stetson, he was young, with a tall, lean body that could only be acquired through hard, physical labor or hours at the gym. And somehow she couldn't see this cowboy stepping his booted feet onto a treadmill or any other piece of gym machinery. No doubt those long, muscular thighs straining against his jeans had developed from hours of straddling a horse. Not a stationary bike.

"Oh, there you are, Stephanie." Dayna walked up to Stephanie and handed her a manila folder with the dog's file. "I'm taking Seymour and his owner to Exam Room 2."

Stephanie glanced over the tall blonde's shoulder to where the cowboy was standing patiently with the leashed dog. As soon as he spotted Stephanie glancing in his direction, he tipped the brim of his hat and grinned.

Oh, Lord, for once in her life, Monica might have been right. This man's looks were lethal!

Clearing her throat, she turned her attention back to Dayna. "Is Dr. Neil ready to see patients? It's a quarter to eight. I thought he'd be starting surgery already."

"Neutering and spaying is on hold for an hour or two. Dr. Neil is running late this morning—some sort of emergency at home. And we have several walk-ins already waiting. Until the doctor gets here I thought you might deal with the less serious patients."

"I'll do my best," Stephanie told her.

With the folder pressed to her chest, Stephanie stepped past Dayna and headed to the exam room. While she waited for the patient and his owner to arrive, she refrained from fidgeting with her clothes or hair. Stephanie had never been one to primp or worry about her appearance and she wasn't about to start just because she was going to meet the sexiest man in Rambling Rose.

She was plucking gloves from a box on a work counter when the door opened and Dayna ushered the man and dog into the examining room. Stephanie instantly felt the oxygen being sucked from the space around her. Either that or her lungs had forgotten how to function.

"Stephanie, this is Acton Donovan," Dayna said, introducing the cowboy. "Acton, this is Stephanie Fortune. She's Dr. Neil's right-hand man."

He cleared his throat and shot another lopsided grin in Stephanie's direction. "Excuse me, Dayna, but she, uh, doesn't look like a man to me."

Dayna glanced at Stephanie's pink face before she turned a suggestive look on the cowboy. "It's just like you to notice, Acton," she said drily. "Stephanie is Dr. Neil's number-one *assistant*. She'll take care of you—I mean, she'll take care of Seymour."

Dayna left the room and after the door had clicked closed behind her, the long, tall cowboy looked at her, his expression a bit sheepish. "Guess you can tell Dayna thinks I'm a pest."

"You two know each other?" Stephanie asked.

"Oh, sure. We went to the same school. Except that she was a few grades ahead of me. She thought I was a pest then, too."

"Oh? Why is that?"

One of his broad shoulders rose and fell and Stephanie's gaze automatically dropped to the front of his shirt. The blue-denim Western shirt molded to the muscular shape of his chest and torso, and for one brief second Stephanie wondered what he looked like beneath the tough fabric.

He chuckled. "I was a bit naughty back in my younger days."

He wasn't exactly old now, she thought. And even from the distance of a few feet, she could see there was a mischievous twinkle in his sky-blue eyes.

Deciding it would be best to drop the subject, she cleared her throat and walked around the examining table to where the spotted black-and-white dog was sitting close to Acton's leg.

"So what brings Seymour to the clinic today?" she asked. "Is he not feeling well?"

"He's having scratching fits. And I can't find a flea or any kind of insect on him."

As though Seymour understood the two humans were discussing him, he looked up at her and whined.

Before Stephanie approached the dog, she asked, "Is he friendly?"

"He's never bitten anyone, but he can have a nasty temper. He snaps at me whenever he wants to remind me that he's the boss. And he isn't good around strangers, and that includes Dr. Neil."

Stephanie wasn't put off by his words of warning. Most cats and dogs wanted to be friends. When they did lash out it was out of fear and the instinct to protect themselves. "Well, I have an idea that Seymour is a very smart guy and he knows I'm going to help him feel better. Don't you, Seymour?"

With her palm upward, she allowed the dog to sniff her hand. Immediately his bushy tail began to thump against the tiled floor. "What a sweet boy," she crooned, then gently stroked his head.

Acton pushed back the brim of his hat and rubbed a hand across his forehead. "Holy smoke! What did you do to him?"

"Just told him I was his friend," Stephanie replied.

She gave the dog another rub between the ears, then patted the end of the examining table. "Would you like to sit up here, Seymour, so I can take a look at you?"

The dog promptly walked over, stood on his hind legs and rested his paws on the edge of the table. Stephanie put her hands beneath his hips and lifted the dog onto the stainless-steel surface.

"Well, if that isn't the damnedest thing I've ever seen!" Acton exclaimed. "I normally have to man-handle him up there and hold him down while Dr. Neil takes care of business. Look at that traitor! He's actually enjoying this!"

Stephanie took her eyes off Seymour long enough to look at his owner, then promptly wished she hadn't. Now that he was standing only an arm's length away from her, she was bowled over by the vivid blue of his eyes and the tanned, masculine angles of his face.

He wasn't one of those pretty boys, she thought. No, there were too many little imperfections about the man to put him in that category. Like the unruly way his sandy blond hair curled around his ears and down the back of his neck, the faint white scar that marked one brown eyebrow, the way the bridge of his nose was a bit too sharp and the jut of his chin overly stubborn. But, dear heaven, put them all together and he had enough sex appeal to knock any woman off her feet.

After drawing in a deep breath, she suggested, "Perhaps you should try a different tactic. Like allowing him to choose to obey rather than forcing him into it."

The eyebrow with the scar arched upward and his reaction had Stephanie wondering if any woman ever dared to question him.

"I could give him an hour to choose to jump on that table and he'd still be sitting on the floor giving me the evil eye. You've put some sort of spell on him. Do you practice magic tricks or something?"

Stephanie turned her attention to the dog, and after checking his vitals, she began a visual inspection of his eyes, nose, teeth and coat.

"I can assure you I haven't put Seymour under any kind of spell. And, no—I'm not a magician. I don't even like magic."

"Uh, what about cowboys with unruly dogs?"

The flirtatious tone of his voice warned her not to look up, but she couldn't stop herself. The boyish grin on his face was worse than charming—it was downright sinful.

"I don't know any cowboys with unruly dogs," she said stiffly.

He laughed. "You do now."

His laughter was infectious and Stephanie had to press her lips tightly together to prevent herself from smiling back at him.

"I only met you five minutes ago. I don't know you."

"Well, we've been properly introduced. And in my case, what you see is what you get."

She didn't plan on getting anything from this man, except a bundle of rattled nerves. Which was so unlike her. She'd been around all sorts of good-looking men before and never experienced this kind of hot, shivery feeling. It was ridiculous.

"I see. No pretense or subterfuge with you," she said as she lifted back one of Seymour's ears to look inside.

"That's right, Miss Fortune. I'm one-hundred-percent genuine."

When Stephanie had first moved to Texas, she'd quickly learned that people put the *Miss* in front of a woman's name to show respect. Especially when they were speaking to an elder. But the way Acton Donovan said "Miss Fortune" made it sound down-right provocative.

"That's nice to know," she replied.

She finished with Seymour's left ear and moved to the right. Across the examining table, she heard

Acton release a long sigh. Whether he was tired, or impatient, or simply bored with her, she couldn't guess.

He said, "If it's any help, he's constantly scratching underneath his neck and his belly."

"What sort of food do you give Seymour? The dry chunks?"

He named a certain brand. "Fed him that ever since he was a tiny pup. That's been four years."

"I've never heard of that brand."

"Get it at the feed-and-grain store where we buy our cattle cubes and everything else we need on the ranch."

She vaguely recalled Monica saying the Donovans owned a ranch north of town. No doubt he was experienced in dealing with large animals like cattle and horses, she thought.

"What color is the food?"

"Excuse me? I didn't know food needed to be color-coordinated with the animal that eats it."

She shot him a droll look. "It's better to be free of food coloring. Some animals are allergic, including dogs."

"Oh. Sorry. Guess that's why you're the doc's right-hand man—I mean…woman. You know a hell of a lot more than I do."

Frowning, she turned her focus back to Seymour.

He shuffled his feet. "Sorry again. I meant to say

heck. As for Seymour's food, it's just plain brown. You think what he eats is making him scratch?"

"If the food doesn't have colored pieces, it's probably fine. But I'm fairly certain he's having an allergic reaction to something. Which could be one thing or many things." She parted the fur on the dog's throat. "See? He has these irritated patches of skin in several places on his throat and underbelly."

Acton lifted his hat from his head and leaned in for a closer look at the dog, which put his face not far from the pretty vet assistant. Immediately, Seymour bared his teeth and gave Acton a warning growl.

"You damned turncoat! I'm not going to touch Miss Stephanie, so just quit your growling."

Stephanie straightened away from him and the dog. "Is this his normal behavior?"

He looked up at her and grinned. "No. He's just acting this way because he's smitten with you and jealous of me. He doesn't want me to get close to you or touch you. See, let me show you."

He reached over and placed his hand on Stephanie's arm, which promptly caused Seymour to erupt in a barking, teeth-gnashing fit.

She swiftly jerked away her arm and stepped back. "I really don't have time for this sort of… demonstration. And I honestly think you ought to leave the room so I can give your dog the treatment he needs."

Up until a few minutes ago, when Dayna had introduced the two of them, he'd never seen Stephanie Fortune. Not here in the clinic or anywhere around Rambling Rose. She didn't exactly have a Texas drawl, nor did she have a Louisianan lilt to her voice. Which meant she'd migrated here from much farther away.

He'd heard about some rich folks by the name of Fortune moving into the huge mansion on the outskirts of town. He'd also read a few articles in the local paper about Fortune Brothers Construction building the pediatric clinic and this animal clinic, but he'd never met any of the family. Acton couldn't imagine this woman being one of them, anyway. Why would someone who belonged to such a wealthy family be working in an animal clinic, handling mutts like Seymour? No, Stephanie must be from a different bunch of Fortunes, he decided.

"Okay, Miss Stephanie, no more demonstrations. I'll be good." To convince her, he moved a few feet away from Seymour and the examining table.

She darted him a wary glance, then let out a long breath and stepped tentatively back to the dog. "Just be sure you stay where you are."

Acton tried not to grin at her, but she looked so darn pretty, with a bright shade of pink splashed across her cheeks and her blue eyes flashing, that he couldn't help himself.

"I won't move a muscle," he promised. "Even if a honeybee flew in here right this minute and landed on my nose, I wouldn't even swat it away. But then, if a honeybee really did fly in here it wouldn't land on me, anyway. It would go straight to you."

A suggestive line like that would normally catch any woman's attention. Apparently Stephanie Fortune wasn't just any woman. Instead of glancing at Acton, she kept her focus firmly on Seymour.

"That's a bunch of nonsense," she said as she continued to part Seymour's long hair and examine his skin.

"Makes plenty of sense to me. Bees go straight to honey and I can tell by the way Seymour takes to you that you're sweet."

She shot him a droll look. "I'm sorry, Mr. Donovan, but this flattery you're throwing at me won't do a thing to lighten your vet bill."

He let out a good-natured groan. "And here I was trying my best to get a free visit this morning. Oh, well, Seymour's worth it."

She stroked the dog's head, then turned to the cabinet, where Seymour's medical file was lying open. As she started writing on one of the pages, she said, "That's good to hear. A loved pet is always a healthier pet."

Acton could've told her that the same went for a

man, too. But he kept the comment to himself. She didn't appear to appreciate his brand of flirting. Which might mean she had a husband or a steady boyfriend.

He'd noticed her left hand was empty of a wedding ring or anything resembling one. But given the nature of her work, she might not wear one while she was dealing with animals. He hoped his assumption was wrong. There was something about the pretty redhead that made it impossible to tear his gaze away from her. Even if she wasn't noticing a thing about him.

While Acton was carefully studying the graceful curve of her waist and hips, she suddenly walked over to the door and partially stepped into the hallway. She must have signaled for Dayna to join her because after a brief moment, Stephanie reentered the room with the other woman right behind her.

"It looks as though Seymour is suffering from allergies," Stephanie explained to Dayna. "And from Dr. Neil's notes, he's treated the dog before with shots."

"So what now?" Acton asked. "Can you give him the medicine he needs or do I need to wait around until Dr. Neil gets here?"

Stephanie looked at him. "I can give him what he's been prescribed before. Or you can wait until Dr. Neil comes."

"And at this point, we don't know when that might be," Dayna interjected.

"I'll take my chances with you, Miss Fortune." He winked at her. "Seymour obviously trusts you."

The serious expression on her face never wavering, she turned to Dayna and instructed her as to what sort of medications she needed for the dog.

"I'll be right back with them," Dayna said, then warned Stephanie, "But while I'm gone don't listen to a word Acton says. He's a wolf disguised in cowboy clothing."

"Aww, Dayna, don't be telling Miss Fortune scary stuff like that. I'll never get her to like me."

"Ha!" Dayna laughed and gave him a backward wave as she hurried out of the examining room.

With Dayna gone, Acton glanced at Stephanie, but her attention was riveted on Seymour. What did a man have to do to get a smile out of the woman? Stand on his head or walk on his hands? Maybe she just didn't like cowboys. The thought bummed him out more than he cared to admit.

"Dayna is joking," he said. "I'm not really a wolf. See? I don't have fangs, at all."

To his delight, she looked up at him and he gave her an extra wide smile to show his teeth.

"I'm quite certain you're not a member of the *Canis lupus* family, Mr. Donovan," she said primly.

He shook his head and wondered why he wanted Stephanie Fortune to notice him. Not as Seymour's owner, but as a man. She wasn't his type at all. He liked fun girls who naturally smiled and laughed. This woman was as serious as a judge.

"No one calls me Mr. Donovan. I'd be pleased if you'd just call me Acton. And if I knew what a *Canis lupus* was, then I might know what you're really thinking about me, uh, being a wolf."

To his surprise, the corners of her mouth lifted with something like amusement. "*Canis lupus* means *dog wolf.*"

"Oh. That's good. Because I'm as gentle as a little pup."

She looked as though she was about to reply to that when Dayna suddenly stepped back into the room carrying a needle, a syringe and a fat jar.

Before Seymour had a clue what was happening, Stephanie had already pulled up the skin on the back of his neck and injected him with the medicine.

"Amazing. Purely amazing," he said with disbelief. "I'd have to chase Seymour all over the county to do that." He looked at Dayna and winked. "Does she put spells on all the animals who come to the clinic?"

"Ninety percent of them," Dayna agreed. "She has the touch."

Stephanie opened the jar of ointment and began to swipe it on the worst of the raw spots on Seymour's skin. "Do you think you can do this twice a day? It will help stop the itching and heal the skin."

"We'll probably end up in a wrestling match, but I'll try."

"Any amount you can manage to put on him will help." She put the lid back on the jar and jumped the dog off the examining table. "Seymour is ready to go home. If he doesn't seem to be improving in a couple of days, then we'll need to see him again."

She handed Seymour's leash and the jar of ointment over to Acton, and with the dog walking alongside him, he followed the two women out of the examining room and back to the waiting area, where a payout counter was located next to the check-in desk.

"Don't wait so long to come see us again, Acton," Dayna said. "We can always use a smiling face around here."

"I have a feeling I'll be back soon." He glanced around to see Stephanie squatted on her heels, giving Seymour a goodbye hug. Too bad he wasn't a dog, Acton thought.

Leaving the dog, she stepped forward and handed an itemized bill to the young woman behind the counter, then turned and extended a hand to him.

He wrapped his hand around hers and was totally enchanted by the incredibly soft skin pressed against his, and the gaze of her deep blue eyes connecting with his. Acton could've stood there until the cows came home. Unfortunately, she had other ideas.

Easing her hand from his, she stepped back. "It was nice meeting you, Acton. I'm glad you brought Seymour to the clinic to be treated. He should feel better soon."

Feeling unusually tongue-tied, he stuttered, "Uh, sure. It was nice meeting you. And thanks for taking care of my dog."

She turned and walked away, but not before the tiny smile on her face smacked Acton right in the middle of his chest. *What in heck was going on here?* he wondered. First she had Seymour eating out of her hand and now he was feeling like a moonstruck teenager.

"Will that be cash or card, Acton?"

The question failed to register with him. He was too busy watching Stephanie leave the waiting area with an older woman toting a cat carrier.

"Acton! Do you think you can beam yourself back to earth?"

Forcing his attention back to the counter, he stared blankly at Sheri, a young woman he'd known since their kindergarten days.

"Sorry, Sheri. Did you say something?"

Sighing, she gave him a smile that would've melted a lesser man's bones. "How do you want to pay your bill today? With cash or card?"

Mentally shaking himself, Acton dug his wallet from the back pocket of his jeans. "Card. How much is it?"

The amount Sheri quoted caused him to whistle under his breath and he glanced wryly down at Seymour. The dog was grinning happily and thumping his bushy tail. Yep, Acton thought, the dog was still under Stephanie Fortune's spell.

"Seymour, I'm not so sure you're worth this," he said. "But I guess I'll keep you."

He swiped the debit card, then punched in his PIN. After he'd placed it back in his wallet, he leaned casually against the counter.

With gamine features and short black hair, Sheri was cute, but in his opinion, not anywhere near as pretty or classy as Stephanie.

"So when did Miss Fortune come to work for Paws and Claws?"

Sheri handed him a receipt. "Before our new clinic opened. She had lots of experience back in Fort Lauderdale, Florida, working with animals, so Dr. Neil hired her right off."

"Hmm, Florida," he mused aloud. "Wonder how she happened to come to Texas?"

Surprised, Sheri asked, "Are you saying you don't know who she is?"

Acton frowned. "Am I supposed to know her?"

She rolled her eyes. "Acton, you really ought to get out of the barn more often. It means Stephanie is one of *the* Fortunes. It also means that she's way out of your league, cowboy."

"Maybe in your mind, Sheri. But I might have other ideas about that."

Grinning at the shocked look on Sheri's face, Acton stuffed the receipt in his shirt pocket and led Seymour out of the clinic.

Chapter Two

"It was more than obvious the cowboy liked you. The way he was looking at you…" Dayna's words ended on a wistful sigh. "If only he would look at me that way, I'd be walking around on a cloud."

Stephanie glanced at her coworker as the two women moved from one kennel to the next, checking on the cats that had been spayed and neutered earlier in the day.

"He? Who are you talking about?"

Dayna rolled her eyes to the ceiling. "Oh, come on, Stephanie. There's only been one hunk of a man stroll into the clinic today. I'm talking about Acton—

the dreamy cowboy. You know! Blond hair, sparkling blue eyes and a grin that turns my knees to mush."

"Oh, him." Shaking her head, Stephanie turned her attention back to the cats. "If you think the man had any interest in me personally, you're totally confused. Anyway, he's obviously a flirt. And I seriously doubt he discriminates by age or looks. He wouldn't have acted any differently if I'd been an eighty-year-old grandmother."

"Oh, puh-leeze! If you believe that nonsense, then you're thinking has gone haywire." Dayna frowned in disbelief. "Didn't you think he was cute and sexy? The whole staff is still going gaga over him."

Stephanie reached into the kennel and rubbed a finger gently down the middle of the head of a calico cat. She loved animals and had ever since she'd been old enough to know what they were. The job she'd held back in Fort Lauderdale had been at an animal clinic such as this one, only larger. She'd enjoyed working there and had been hesitant about giving it up to move here to Texas. But her three brothers had assured her she wouldn't have any trouble finding an equally worthwhile job. And they'd been right. So far, working for Dr. Neil had been a real pleasure.

As for having a man in her life, that was an entirely different matter. She'd been burned too many times to let a young hunk like Acton Donovan turn her head.

"Okay, I'll admit the guy was super cute and

sexy—in a boyish way. Rather young, though," Stephanie told her, then cast a curious glance at the other woman. "Does he, uh, have a steady girl-friend?"

Dayna laughed as though her question was the funniest thing she'd heard in a long time. "Let me put it this way—Acton has a steady stream of girl-friends. In the plural sense." She named several different young women who'd recently brought their pets to the clinic. "Those are a few of his castoffs."

Somehow that tidbit of information didn't surprise Stephanie. The man had reeked of charm and sexi-ness. He probably had a bevy of women knocking on his door. Which made the idea of him being in-terested in Stephanie even more ridiculous and her more determined to forget him. Her last boyfriend, the one she thought she wanted to spend the rest of her life with, had been a playboy. Only Stephanie hadn't known it until her heart had become involved. Then she'd found out the hard way that he was see-ing other women on the side.

"I see," she said thoughtfully. "So I guess you'd say he's a playboy in boots and hat."

"That's one way of putting it. But I'm sure every woman who goes out with him likes to believe she's the one who can settle him down—turn him into a husband and daddy," Dayna told her.

Stephanie couldn't picture Acton Donovan set-tling down in the near future or even years from now.

And she figured any woman who tried to transform him would only be asking for heartache.

"Well, the guy seemed nice enough. But I'm not interested. Not only is he too young and too much of a flirt for my taste, but there's only one man I'm interested in. My little man, Linus. He's my main focus right now."

"That's well and good. But you might not always have Linus in your life. Even if his mother never comes back, there's a dad out there somewhere."

That thought was something Stephanie tried not to dwell on. "That's the reality I live with every day, Dayna. Although, Laurel told my sister-in-law, Becky, that the baby's father was totally out of the picture."

"Yes, that's what this Laurel woman said. But can anyone really believe her? What kind of woman gives birth to a baby and only days later, leaves it at the front desk of the Rambling Rose Pediatric Center?"

Stephanie moved on to another kennel with Dayna following close behind her. "From what everyone who was at the ribbon-cutting ceremony at the center says, Laurel seemed perfectly fine when she went into labor. But who knows? She was just a stranger passing through. She could've made up the part about the father. All I know is that I love the little guy like he's my own. And right now I'm concentrating on him. I'm just not interested in dating anyone."

"Well, I'll say one thing," Dayna replied. "If you

can resist Acton, then I'm going to start calling you Lady of Steel."

Stephanie laughed. "Come on, it's almost closing time. We'd better make sure everything is ready to shut down before Dr. Neil locks the doors for the night."

Later that evening, Acton was cleaning up the mess he'd made cooking his supper when he heard a knock on the front door.

After drying his hands on a dish towel, he walked through the small house where his grandparents used to live and peeked through the curtain covering the paned window on the door.

Seeing his oldest brother, Shawn, standing on the porch, Acton pulled open the door.

"What the heck are you doing knocking?" Acton asked him. "You know you can just open the door and come on in."

Shawn, who was similar to Acton in coloring, but a bit taller, cast his brother a droll look. "And walk in on you and some lady in a lip-lock or something worse? No thanks. I'll keep knocking."

Up until a couple of months ago, Acton had lived in the big ranch house with his parents and two brothers. But then his father, Ramsey, had decided that his own mother, Hatti, no longer needed to be living here alone and had practically ordered her to move into the big house. Seeing the chance to have a place of his own, Acton had promptly made the move.

Stepping into the living room, Shawn gestured to the apron tied around Acton's waist. "What are you doing, anyway? Don't tell me you're trying to cook."

Acton closed the door behind him. "I'm cleaning up my mess. And who are you kidding? You know I'm a pretty darn good cook. When it comes to making great dishes, Grandma Hatti is a good teacher. I made spaghetti. Want some?"

"No thanks. I had a burger in town. But I will take some coffee. Got any made?"

"No. But it'll just take a minute to get some brewing."

The two men passed through the living room, down a short hallway, then into a small kitchen decorated in red, green and white.

Shawn pulled out a chair at a round pine table and sank into it. "Actually, I didn't come by to beg for a cup of coffee. I came by to tell you that Dad has decided to work the herd in the northwest corner in the morning. He wants to be loading the portable pens by daybreak."

"I hope he doesn't plan on doing all three hundred head in one day," Acton said. "Has he hired any day help?"

Shawn shook his head. "He said if four grown men can't handle the job, then he needs to get rid of some cattle."

Acton groaned as he spooned coffee grounds into a filtered basket. "Sounds like we're in for a long day tomorrow."

"That's why I stopped by. To make sure you didn't have something else planned."

"Like what?" Acton took a seat at the opposite end of the table. "I show up every day for work, don't I?"

"Well, you've been known to get distracted by a pretty face." He eyed Acton's ragged blue jeans and old gray T-shirt. "You're not going out tonight?"

Acton frowned. "On a date, you mean?"

"Yes. Like you and a girl," Shawn said drily.

"No. I wished I was," Acton admitted. "But I wasn't sure the girl would agree to going out with me. So I didn't ask."

Shawn's eyebrows piqued with curiosity. "Don't tell me you ran in to a woman who actually resisted your charm."

Acton grunted with wry humor. "She resisted me, all right. To be honest, I don't even think she liked me. She was polite enough. But I think that's because it was her job."

"Hmm. Do I know this lady?"

Acton shrugged. "I doubt it. She's moved here from Florida and works for Dr. Neil at Paws and Claws as a vet assistant. I took Seymour there this morning to get something done about his scratching."

"From Florida..." Shawn mused. "What's her name?"

"Fortune. Stephanie Fortune."

Shawn let out a disbelieving groan. "Oh, dear brother, now I understand why you didn't get to first base with her. She's probably one of the Fortunes that moved here a few months ago. You know, the ones who moved into that mansion on the outskirts of town. I think they call it the Fame and Fortune Ranch or something. Other than a few horses, I don't believe there are actually any livestock on the place. But you know how city folks are. They own a few acres in the country and get the idea that entitles them to call it a ranch."

"Oh, so that's what Sheri meant when she said Stephanie was one of 'the' Fortunes," he remarked. "Obviously these people are rich."

Shawn shrugged one of his broad shoulders. "Well, it appears so. Fortune Brothers Construction is the company that finished the pediatric center and the animal clinic. Now they're working on some other properties in town. So apparently, they have money. And I heard tell that they're related to the famous Fortune family in Austin."

Seeing the coffee had finished dripping, Acton rose from his seat and poured two cups.

"I have some pecan pie. Want a piece?"

"Don't tell me you baked a pie," Shawn told him. "I won't believe it."

"Ha! Grandma was pretty good at teaching me

how to cook, but she wasn't that good. The pie came straight out of the bakery in the grocery store."

"In that case, I'll eat some."

Acton cut two pieces of the dessert and carried everything over to the table.

Once they were both eating, Acton said, "Dr. Neil wasn't at the clinic this morning so Stephanie treated Seymour."

"Bet that was a wrestling match. No wonder she wasn't interested in you, after she had to deal with that rowdy dog of yours."

"Wrong, brother. Seymour was a perfect gentleman. He took to Stephanie like…well, I never saw anything like it. She could have told him to walk across the exam room on his hind feet and he would've done it for her."

"Hmm. That's a first. Frankly, it surprises me that this Fortune woman was working in a place like Paws and Claws. Dealing with sick and wounded animals all day isn't exactly what I'd consider a glamorous job."

"Stephanie doesn't seem like the glamorous sort. But she sure is pretty. And she didn't act uppity. Just a bit disinterested—in me."

"Aww, my poor little brother. He finally met a female he couldn't charm out of her shoes," Shawn teased. "Sounds like trouble ahead for you."

Acton frowned at his brother. "Trouble? A sweet

little thing like Stephanie couldn't cause trouble. Not with me."

Shawn snorted. "Maybe in another five years you'll learn about women."

Acton let out a short laugh. "Like you're an expert on females? Cows, maybe. But not pretty women."

"Well, I have sense enough to know that a woman, pretty or homely, isn't going to ever be serious about a simple cowboy. Men like us can't offer a woman riches."

"Not all women want riches," he retorted.

Shawn's response to that was a dry laugh. "Dream on, brother."

Acton thought as he sliced off a bite of pie. "I guess this Fortune family must have tons of money. From a distance, that house of theirs looks impressive."

"I wouldn't call it a house. It's a mansion."

"Well, by Texas standards, it's not the biggest or the best. But it's hardly a shack," Acton joked.

"I can bet you one thing," Shawn said. "Stephanie Fortune's kitchen doesn't look like this one. I doubt she's ever so much as cooked herself an egg."

Acton could've told his brother he wasn't looking for a cook, but he kept the remark to himself. He didn't want Shawn or any of his family to get the idea that he was looking for one special woman. Their parents had already been hounding their three sons to settle down and give them more grandchildren.

Acton said, "I think I recall reading an opinion piece in the paper about Fortune Brothers Construction. Some of the folks in Rambling Rose aren't too happy about these fancy new buildings and shops they're planning for the town."

Shawn shrugged. "You know how some of the older townsfolk are. They're not keen on change. Especially the progressive kind. Frankly, I think it's good to make improvements."

"I get that part of it," Acton acknowledged. "But I agree with the old folks about not wanting to turn Rambling Rose into some sort of tourist attraction. Hell, pretty soon it will be against the law to ride our horses down Main Street."

Shaking his head, Shawn snickered. "Acton, since when have you ridden your horse down Main Street? Not since us three brothers decided to ride in the rodeo parade and that was five years ago!"

Acton carried his empty plate over to the sink, then refilled his coffee cup. "I'm only using that as an example of how things are changing around here."

"Well, if you want to get to first base with Stephanie Fortune, then I suggest you don't bring up the subject of her brothers' plans for a ritzy hotel."

Acton glanced at his brother. "A ritzy hotel? For real?"

"That's what I'm hearing. But you can hear anything at the Crockett Café."

The old eating establishment had been a fixture

in Rambling Rose for as long as Acton could remember. When he and Shawn and their brother Danny had been small boys, their father would take them to the café on the weekend as a special treat for doing their chores. All three would get milk shakes. The kind that was handmade with real ice cream and so thick you had to eat it with a spoon. The café still made handmade milk shakes, but now that Acton and his brothers were all grown men, it wasn't the same.

"A ritzy hotel in Rambling Rose," he murmured, thinking aloud. "Don't reckon that will ever work. But you can bet I won't tell Stephanie Fortune my opinion on the subject—if I ever get the chance."

Finished with the pie, Shawn pushed aside his plate and cast a taunting grin at Acton. "How do you plan on seeing her again? You going to take Seymour back for a special checkup?"

"If he doesn't improve I'm supposed to take him back. Damn dog, I don't think he's scratched once since I got him home. So I doubt I can use him for an excuse."

Clearly amused, Shawn said, "You can always gather up the barn cats and take them in for their yearly shots."

"Dad always takes care of that chore," Acton said, then snapped his fingers with sudden dawning. "I know. I'll take Elizabeth and Ryan by Paws and Claws. The clinic always has a few cats and dogs to be adopted and the kids love to look at them."

Elizabeth, age seven, and nine-year-old Ryan were their older sister's kids. On some evenings, after Acton was finished with his ranch chores, he'd drive over to Gina's house and take the kids out for burgers or pizza. Gina often accused Acton of spoiling her children, but to tell the truth, he probably enjoyed the outings as much, or more, than the kids.

"Oh, how low can you stoop, Acton? Using your own niece and nephew to snag the attention of a woman," Shawn taunted jokingly.

Frowning now, Acton walked back over to the table. "Look who's talking. I don't see you making any headway in the love department."

Shawn's eyebrows shot up. "Love? Don't try to tell me that's what you looking for."

Acton could feel his face growing hot and he figured he looked like a sun-ripened tomato. Damn it, there were times Shawn could make him feel like he was sixteen years old again.

"Well, what if I am?" He tossed the question at his big brother. "Is there anything wrong with that?"

The goading look on Shawn's face turned empathetic. "No. Nothing wrong at all. Except that maybe..."

His words trailed away and Acton couldn't let it go at that. In spite of the teasing and bantering that went on between him and his brothers, Acton valued their thoughts and opinions.

"Except what?" Acton prodded him to answer.

Shawn shrugged. "That maybe when you really start looking for a woman to love, you should start with someone in your own social sphere. Just my opinion, little brother."

If Acton was being totally honest, he'd probably admit that Shawn was right. Wanting to date someone out of his league was one thing, but getting serious about her would be downright stupid.

"Don't worry. I'm not hearing wedding bells in my head. That's not going to happen for another ten years, at least."

Shawn chuckled. "I won't tell Mom and Dad. They have the idea that you moved down here to Grandma's house because you have marriage on your mind."

Acton let out a loud burst of laughter. "Seriously? Who would I be marrying?"

Shawn pretended to think. "Well, you've been seeing the little blonde who works at Reddick's Ranch Supply on a fairly regular basis."

Acton's laughter quieted to a chuckle. "Marietta? I've already put the brakes on dating her. She's too much of a party girl."

His comment caused Shawn to stare at him in comical disbelief. "Too much of a party girl? For you? Is that possible?"

"It is when she's partying with more than me."

"Oh."

"Yeah. Oh. Which is no big deal. We didn't have

a serious thing going. And I sure didn't move down here to Grandma's house because of Marietta. I moved to give everyone more space in the big house."

"Oh, I thought you moved because you were tired of everybody treating you like the baby of the family. That you wanted to prove you can take care of yourself."

Acton slanted him a perceptive glance. "Maybe that, too, big brother."

Stephanie softly hummed a lullaby as she gently rocked Linus and watched the last of the formula in the bottle drain away. In spite of the baby being born a bit early, he was thriving. This past month his cheeks had rounded and his arms and legs had grown fleshier. She'd even noticed that his gaze was trying more and more to focus on her face.

Incredibly, Stephanie had ended up being Linus's foster mother by sheer happenstance. When Laurel had staggered into the ribbon-cutting ceremony in the throes of labor and shouted for help, Stephanie's sister-in-law, Becky, who happened to be a nurse, and Dr. Green both rushed to the frantic woman's aid. The next day, after the news had spread that she and the baby were safely settled in a hospital in San Antonio, everyone had believed that was the last they'd ever hear of the incident.

But a couple weeks later, Laurel had walked into the pediatric center, handed over the baby to a nurse and declared she couldn't handle being a parent. Later, they'd found a note on the baby stating his rightful home would be found at Fortune's Foundling Hospital.

Neither Laurel's behavior nor the note had made any sense. And to make matters worse, none of the local foster families had been able to take in the infant they'd initially called Baby L. Stephanie, however, had.

Her brothers, Callum, Dillon and Steven, had been surprised. They'd always known she was a nurturer with a soft heart. However, they had been stunned to learn that she'd already gone through the process of being fingerprinted and background-checked in hopes of adopting one day.

They had all wondered why their lovely sister needed to adopt a child when she could give birth to one of her own. Stephanie hadn't bothered to explain her reasons. They might not want to admit it, but all three brothers knew the answer to that question. Over the past few years they'd watched her suffer through several short-lived relationships, none of which had even gotten close to true love or an engagement ring. She didn't want to wait to start a family at the end of her childbearing years. She wanted to have children while she was still young. And hopefully, later on, she might be fortunate enough to find a man who would truly love her.

"Linus, you might be the only baby I'll ever have

a chance to hold and cherish," she whispered down to the sleeping boy.

His lips had gone slack around the nipple, and as Stephanie carefully eased the bottle from his mouth, emotional tears stung her eyes. She'd been told that in a year's time if neither parent showed up to claim the boy, she might have a chance to adopt him. But a year was a long time. Anything could happen between now and then.

She rose from the cushioned rocker, then carried Linus over to a hooded bassinet and was tucking a warm blanket around him when a knock sounded on the door of her suite at the Fame and Fortune Ranch.

After crossing the large space that served as a living room, she opened the door to find Steven, her oldest brother, holding a large covered tray.

"Room service," he said cheerily. "Hungry?"

She pulled the door wide and gestured for him to come in. "I was about to come down to the kitchen to see if there was anything to eat. What's all that?" she asked, gesturing to the tray. "I thought Manny was taking the night off."

He carried the loaded tray over to a green leather couch and placed it on a glass-and-wood coffee table. As Stephanie followed her brother, she thought she caught a whiff of pizza.

"Callum treated the construction crew this evening and there was so much food left over I brought some home."

"This is nice, Steven. Thanks for thinking of me."

"When you didn't come down to dinner, I thought I'd better check on you. Is everything okay?"

For a long while in their family, Stephanie had been the only girl and her four older brothers had been very protective of their little sister. And even though a set of triplet girls had been born into the family four years after Stephanie, the guys still went out of their way to shield and care for her. Maybe because they thought that, due to her bad luck at love, she might never have a husband to love and protect her.

She smiled at Steven, while hoping that the tears that had stung her eyes a few moments ago were no longer visible. "Sure. Everything is fine. We had a hectic day at the clinic and it was later than usual when I finally picked up Linus from day care. So I've been playing catch-up. By the time I took care of my pets, Linus was yelling that he was hungry. So I put supper on hold."

Steven chuckled. "I'd be flat on the floor if I'd been that busy today."

She gave a wry laugh, then took a seat on the couch. "Join me?"

"I'll sit for a minute. But I can't stay for long. Callum is on a conference call and wants to talk with me afterward."

"Callum is really excited about his projects. I think even more so now that Becky and the children are in his life." She was happy for her brother; he'd found a wonderful single mother of twins who'd given him an instant family. She glanced slyly at her brother. "Is seeing him so happy giving you any ideas to become a family man?"

Steven shrugged. "It'll take more than Callum's grinning face to get me to the altar."

Stephanie pulled the linen cloth from the tray to expose a wide array of food, ranging from hot wings and pizza, to macaroni and cheese and chocolate cake.

"No salad?" she asked teasingly.

Steven chuckled. "Sorry. The guys ate all the salad. There wasn't a drop of it left."

"I'd be willing to bet there wasn't a drop of it to begin with," she said drily.

He laughed. "Construction workers need more than rabbit food for their dinner." He glanced around him. "Speaking of rabbits, where is Orville?"

"Look behind you. He finally managed to charm Violet and Daisy into sharing their bed."

Steven glanced behind the couch to see Stephanie's Siamese cat and yellow tabby snuggled in a large basket. Wedged between the two felines, a brown-and-white domestic rabbit snoozed contentedly.

"Ha! They must have decided Orville was just a strange-looking cat. I'll say one thing—he's one lucky rabbit to have you adopt him. Did you ever find out how he happened to be roaming around the clinic parking lot?"

Stephanie shook her head as she placed a pair of hot wings on a small paper plate. "No. We figure someone just didn't want him anymore and put him there hoping the clinic would take care of him. It's so sad, too, because Orville is a real sweetheart."

"Every needy creature is a sweetheart to you." Steven settled back against the couch and crossed his ankles out in front of him. "Stephanie, sometimes I think you'd take on a small zoo and a dozen kids without ever batting an eye."

Smiling wanly, she shrugged. "What would I be doing if I wasn't taking care of Linus, my pets and the animals at Paws and Claws?"

"Anything you wanted. You might actually have time for a personal life."

Trying not to grimace, Stephanie reached for a piece of cheese pizza. "If you're talking about me getting myself a man, there's no need for you to worry. I've decided the best thing I could ever do for myself is cross marriage off my list of lifelong endeavors."

Steven hardly looked pleased. "You're twenty-seven, intelligent, beautiful and, most of all, loving. But you want to hide away and waste yourself just because you've dated a few losers."

Stephanie ate a bite of pizza before she bothered to reply. "Not only were they losers, they were users and jerks, too. Let's face it, I wouldn't know a good man if he wore a sign around his neck."

"If he has to wear a sign around his neck to let people know he's good, then he probably isn't."

She let out a brittle laugh. "No need to worry, Steven. Linus keeps me happy."

Her brother left the couch and walked over to the bassinet where Linus was sleeping peacefully. Gazing down at the baby, he said, "You're very brave, Stephanie, for taking on this little fellow with so much uncertainty surrounding him."

Leaving her plate on the coffee table, she walked over to where he stood and slipped an arm through his. "I'm hardly brave."

He looked at her. "Don't suppose you've heard any news about the mother?"

"No. It's like her trail has vanished."

The cell phone in his shirt pocket suddenly chirped to signal a new text message had arrived. Steven glanced at the phone. "Callum is finished with his conference call. I'd better go see what he's stirring up next. We've just put the finishing touches on The Shoppes at Rambling Rose."

"Poor you," she said with a grin. "The building never stops."

"Wait until he hears I need to hire more carpenters," he joked. Then he planted a kiss on the top of Stephanie's head and started out of the room.

"Thanks for the food," she called after him.

He gave her a backhanded wave and shut the door behind him.

Stephanie's attention returned to the baby, and as she gazed down at Linus's quiet features, her heart overflowed with warm, maternal love. Would she ever have a child of her own? A man to love?

Love.

These days she rarely allowed herself to dwell on the fleeting emotion. But after meeting Acton Donovan this morning, she'd been feeling totally out of character.

True, she wasn't good at judging the quality of a man, but even she could see he was far from her type.

So why had she continued to think of him throughout the day? Why was she thinking of him now?

Because no guy like him had ever flirted with her? Of course, she'd had men hit on her before, but most of them had been sleazy or unattractive, or just downright obnoxious. But Acton had been none of those things. He'd been cute and rather sweet, and she'd gotten the impression that he was a nice guy. With a dog like Seymour, he had to be nice, she thought.

There you go, Stephanie, judging a man by his dog. That's a brilliant deduction. It's no wonder you've had your heart broken a dozen times. Before long you'll be saying the denim shirt he was wearing made him look dependable and trustworthy.

The mocking voice in her head made her turn

from the bassinet and return to the tray of food sitting on the coffee table.

She couldn't let thoughts of a young, happy-go-lucky cowboy elbow their way in on her common sense. And yet, she couldn't help but wonder what it would be like to have Acton Donovan sitting next to her on the couch, sharing this little supper with her.

Chapter Three

Two days later, with Elizabeth and Ryan safely buckled in the backseat of his truck, Acton was driving to Paws and Claws with one thing on his mind—seeing Stephanie again.

"Why do we have to go to the animal clinic first, Uncle Acton?" Ryan asked. "I'm hungry now."

Elizabeth made a smirking face at her big brother. "You're always hungry. And you can eat any ol' time. We're going to look at the cats first. Mom says if I see a cat I like I can bring it home. 'Cause we don't have Tinker anymore."

"She didn't say that!" Ryan insisted, correcting her. "She said maybe."

"You're lying! She said yes! Not maybe," Elizabeth countered.

"Okay, you two, if you don't be nice to each other, I'm going to turn the truck around and take you both home," Acton warned. "There won't be any cats or burgers or anything else for either of you."

The interior of the truck went silent and a glance in the rearview mirror showed the pair exchanging stunned looks.

"Okay," Ryan mumbled. "If Elizabeth will be nice, I will be, too."

The girl pursed her lips together, and for a moment Acton thought she was going to reach over and bop her brother over the head, but then she smiled to signify all was forgiven.

"I'll be nice, too," she promised.

"I'm glad to hear it," Acton told them. "Because I want you two to be on your best behavior."

"How come?" Ryan asked.

"Because you're supposed to be well-behaved and I have friends at Paws and Claws. I don't want them thinking my sister has raised a pair of heathens."

Puzzled, Elizabeth looked at her brother. "What's 'heathens'?"

"Aww, Lizzie, you know. It means somebody like Mikey Walters."

Elizabeth nodded as though that explained everything. "Oh, so a heathen is a bully and a creep."

"That's one way of putting it," Acton told her, while trying to keep a straight face.

He wheeled the truck into the parking lot of the new Paws and Claws building and after giving the kids one last list of rules to follow, ushered them through the front door of the facility.

With only an hour to go before closing time, there were only two patients left in the waiting room. Both were leashed dogs, who appeared as bored as their owners.

Carla, a young woman with brown hair wrapped into a ballerina bun, waved from behind the check-in desk. "Hi, Acton. Can I help you?"

With a hand on each child's shoulder, he nudged them forward. "This is my niece and nephew. They'd like to look at the cats you have up for adoption."

The attractive receptionist shot him a dazzling smile, while at the desk down from her, Sheri was loudly clearing her throat.

"Dayna might be free at the moment," Sheri said. "Want me to call her?"

Before Carla could make any kind of response, Acton asked, "What about Stephanie? Is she around?"

"She is," Carla said. "But she's assisting Dr. Neil out back with a large animal. A bull with a bad horn or something."

Acton couldn't imagine delicate Stephanie any-where near a bull. But she'd probably put the same charming hex on it like she'd used on Seymour, he thought.

He was about to tell Carla that they'd wait for Stephanie when the door leading back to the examining rooms suddenly opened and a big burly man with a crumpled straw hat and muddy boots entered the room with Stephanie following close behind him.

"There she is now," Carla said. "If you and the kids would like to wait—"

"We will," Acton said before she could finish, then guided his niece and nephew to the nearest couch.

Once the man had dealt with his bill and was leaving the office, Acton hurried the kids over to where Stephanie remained at the checkout desk.

As soon as she spotted him, she smiled and Acton felt something in the middle of his chest melt like a chunk of ice on a hot sidewalk.

"Hello, Mr. Donovan," she said, her gaze encompassing the children standing next to him. "Who are your friends?"

Acton nudged the children slightly forward. "This is my niece, Elizabeth, and my nephew, Ryan."

The smile on her face deepened as she politely shook hands with both children. "Hello, I'm Stephanie. I took care of your uncle's dog for him the other day."

Ryan grinned naughtily. "You mean Seymour? Bet that was a big dogfight."

She arched an eyebrow at Acton. "This boy must spend a lot of time with you."

Acton chuckled. "Everyone says he takes after me. Much to my sister's disappointment."

"Uncle Acton is going to take us to eat. But we want to see the cats first," Elizabeth told her. "The ones that people can take home with them."

Stephanie glanced at Acton again and as he looked at her lovely face, he realized that somehow during the last two days, he'd forgotten just how vibrant her eyes were and how her hair was the color of a red-gold sunset.

"You want to adopt a cat?" she asked him. "That's wonderful."

"Uh, well, not me. I mean, I love cats. I think they're super. But Gina—that's my sister—has promised the kids they can have another cat. The cat they had went missing."

Realizing Ryan was tugging on his sleeve, he looked questioningly down at the boy.

"What about the dogs, Uncle Acton?"

Acton shot Stephanie an apologetic smile. "Sorry. He wants to see the dogs, too. But if you're too busy—"

"Not at all. Dr. Neil just finished with his last patient," she assured him. "You three, follow me."

With Stephanie leading the way, they walked to a room located near the back of the building.

"This is what we call our cat room," she said as she gestured for them to step inside.

"That took some real original thinking," Acton joked.

The room was filled with scratching poles, gym sets and other feline furniture. Stuffed mice, small rolling balls and other toys littered the floor.

"Well, I suppose it could be called the feline room."

"Wow! This is cat heaven, Uncle Acton!" Elizabeth exclaimed. "May I go look in the cages?"

"Of course," Stephanie told her. "But I wouldn't try petting the cats that are running lose. Sometimes they get frightened of strangers and scratch."

"I won't," Elizabeth promised, then rushed over to a cage where a calico mother with a litter of four was housed. Ryan followed close on her heels.

Acton said, "Thank you, Stephanie. This means a lot to the kids, especially Lizzie. She cried for days over her missing Tinker."

"Aww. I can only imagine. I have two cats, two dogs and a rabbit. If any one of them went missing, I'd be devastated."

Surprised, he looked at her. "After working here all day, you go home to five pets? You must really love animals."

"I do love them. When I was a child I couldn't have pets because of my mother's health issues. Since then I've made up for it." A tentative smile played at the corners of her lips. "So how is Seymour? You didn't bring him with you today, so I'm assuming he's doing better."

Acton nodded. "I don't think he's scratched once since I took him home. Yesterday he helped us round up cattle, so he was a happy dog. Today he's resting."

A look of interest brightened her face. "Seymour is a working dog?"

"Why, sure. You don't think I'd keep a mutt like him around just for the company, do you? Damn dog would just as soon snap my hand off as look at me."

She responded with a soft laugh and the sweet sound nearly knocked Acton off his feet.

"What's so funny about that?" he asked, while savoring the fact that he'd somehow managed to make her laugh.

"You thinking Seymour is cranky. He knows how you feel about him. That's why he treats you like—"

"A dog," Acton said, finishing for her. Then he grinned to soften his words. "That's okay. He and I understand each other. And I wouldn't trade him for anything."

"Uncle Acton, come look at this cat! He has stripes that go sideways!" Ryan called out. "Can we have him?"

"But I want this white one!" Elizabeth interjected as she gazed into a separate kennel. "Her ears have black on the tips. She's beautiful!"

Acton glanced at Stephanie. "I think I hear an argument coming on."

"Perhaps their mother would let them have both?" Stephanie suggested. "It would be good for the cats to have a companion."

He contemplated the idea for a moment before he said, "I have a feeling you could talk Gina into it. If I get her on the phone, would you mind speaking to her?"

"I'd be glad to," Stephanie told him.

Acton pulled out his cell phone and punched in his sister's number. To his relief, she answered after the first ring.

"Gina, there's a very nice lady here at Paws and Claws who'd like to speak with you," he told her, then immediately passed the phone to Stephanie.

While the two women discussed the cats, Acton went over to the children. So far, neither had given an inch as to which cat they wanted to take home.

"Uncle Acton, why should Ryan get to choose? He didn't even want to look at the cats. All he's been talking about is dogs!"

"Well, I like dogs, too," Ryan said, attempting to defend himself. "But Mom won't let me have one until we get a yard fence. So a cat would be the next best thing."

Acton rubbed a hand on top of each child's head. "Okay, kids, no arguments, remember?"

They both nodded soberly and Acton kept his smug smile to himself.

"I got a little surprise," he announced. "Miss Stephanie is on the phone right now trying to talk your mother into allowing you both to have a cat. How's that?"

"Oh, that's cool!" Ryan exclaimed.

Elizabeth jumped up and down. "Wow, wow! Triple wow!"

Both kids were hugging Acton's waist when Stephanie walked over and handed him the phone. From the stoic look on her face, he had no idea how the conversation with Gina had turned out.

"So what's the verdict?" he asked.

Stephanie suddenly encompassed all three of them with a happy smile. "She's agreed to letting you have both cats. Only because I told her that you two looked like responsible children who will take proper care of your pets. Am I right?"

"Yeah!" Ryan answered enthusiastically.

Her little features suddenly serious, Elizabeth said, "We're responsible, Miss Stephanie. We're not heathens."

Acton watched Stephanie's mouth fall open just before she covered it with her hand. Whether she was shocked or laughing at Elizabeth's remark, he couldn't tell. He hoped it was the latter.

"Uh, that's a new word she learned," Acton explained.

Turning away from the children, Stephanie dropped her hand, and he was immensely relieved to see she was smiling.

"I wonder where she might've heard it."

The shrewd look on her face very nearly made Acton laugh, and he suddenly realized that Stephanie Fortune was a whole lot more than a pretty face and a shapely figure. Just being in her presence and listening to her soft voice was a pleasure he'd never quite experienced before.

"They're seven and nine years old, and I still haven't learned that they pick up on everything I say," Acton admitted, then gestured toward the caged cats. "I realize it's nearly closing time for the clinic. It might be better to come back tomorrow evening to pick up the cats. That way I can take the kids to the pet store and buy whatever supplies they'll need."

"Sounds good," she said. "I'll have Sheri fill out the adoption papers tomorrow and meanwhile we'll tag both cats so that no one else can take them."

Acton explained the plan to the kids and though they were initially disappointed that they couldn't take the cats with them this evening, neither put up a fuss.

"Does this mean we can go eat now?" Ryan asked.

"I don't want to eat," Elizabeth said. "I want to go to the pet store."

Acton shook his head. "No pet store tonight. We're going to eat."

The girl suddenly looked at Stephanie. "Will you come eat burgers with us, Miss Stephanie? It would be more fun if you would come, too."

Stephanie looked awkwardly over at Acton and his heart skipped a hopeful beat. Did he honestly have a chance in talking her into joining them?

"I wasn't invited," she told Elizabeth.

Tilting her head to one side, the girl said, "I'm inviting you."

"Yes, and that's very nice. But your uncle hasn't invited me. And I—"

"I'm asking you now," Acton interrupted. "Would you like to join us? We're only going down the street to the burger place. The one with the kiddie playground in the front. That is, if you don't have other plans."

For a long moment she appeared to consider his offer, then a slow smile tilted her lips. "Actually, the only plan I have is to go pick up my baby."

Stephanie expected her announcement to surprise Acton, but his friendly expression didn't change. Still, she couldn't help but wonder what he was actually thinking. That she was an unwed mother or a divorcee with a child, or even a widow?

It didn't matter what he was thinking, Stephanie scolded herself. Acton Donovan was just a guy offering her a hamburger, not a red-hot affair.

"You, uh, have a baby?" he asked. "As in a little human baby? Not an animal baby?"

Stephanie couldn't hold back her laughter. "Linus is a real little human baby. He's a month old and I'm his foster mother."

He smiled. "Foster mother? Oh, that's, uh, great. Real great!"

Great for her, or Linus, or the both of them? Stephanie wasn't sure what he meant, but at least the news that she had a baby, even on a temporary basis, hadn't sent him running out the door.

"Yes, well, I really need to pick him up before I could join you three. Unless a baby would bother you," she added, while carefully trying to gauge his reaction. If Linus wasn't welcome, then she'd decline his invitation.

"Bother me? Shoot, no!" He gestured to Elizabeth and Ryan. "I've been around these two since they were a day old. I'm an old hand with babies."

Honestly? He looked more like he was an old hand at creating babies rather than caring for them, Stephanie thought. But she could be wrong about the man. And it wasn't fair for her to be judging him without really knowing him.

She pushed back the cuff of her thin sweater. "It will be a few more minutes before the clinic closes and I can pick up Linus from day care. Elizabeth and Ryan might not want to wait for me."

"We don't mind," Ryan said.

Elizabeth bounced joyfully on her toes. "We won't eat without you, Miss Stephanie. Promise!"

The grin on Acton's face said he didn't mind waiting, either, and the idea that he might actually want Stephanie's company made her feel light hearted and foolishly romantic.

"The kids want you to join us and so do I. Waiting isn't a problem. We'll meet you there."

"Okay. I'll see you there."

He gathered up the children and ushered them out of the cat room. As the door shut behind the trio, Stephanie felt like she'd just encountered one of those Texas whirlwinds she'd heard about. Had she just agreed to a date with Acton Donovan? The gorgeous hunk that made the whole staff at Paws and Claws swoon?

No. It isn't a date, Stephanie. It's sharing some fast food with new friends. A man like Acton will never want a real date with you. So quit daydreaming. You have work to do.

Galvanized by the taunting voice in her head, Stephanie hurried down the hallway to where Dayna was straightening shelves in the supply room.

The woman gave her a sly look. "Sounds like you made a score with Acton."

"What?" Stephanie blurted.

Had her coworker already heard that Stephanie was meeting Acton later? She hoped not. She was hardly ready to start fielding off a bunch of silly questions.

"The cats," Dayna explained. "Acton told us the kids are adopting two of the cats. Good job, Steph."

Stephanie felt a blush sting her face. "I really had nothing to do with that. The cats sold themselves."

Dayna hardly looked convinced. "Carla said when Acton and the kids first came in he was purposely asking for you. Wonder why?"

Stephanie refused to make a big deal over Acton's attention. Especially when she knew his interest would quickly wane. "Probably because he thinks I have some sort of mystical powers with animals."

Dayna laughed. "You do."

Relieved that Dayna accepted her theory, Stephanie quickly changed the subject. "Are all the patients cleared out?"

"Dr. Neil finished with the last one a few minutes ago," Dayna answered. "Let's finish tidying up so we can get out of here."

It took Stephanie another thirty minutes to finish her work at the animal clinic, pick up Linus and drive back to the fast-food restaurant.

When she stepped inside the busy eatery with the baby tucked safely in her arms, she was acutely aware of her stained work jeans and limp hair. She didn't need a mirror to tell her she looked washed out, even though she had taken the time to swipe on a bit of pale pink lipstick.

She was glancing around the room, trying to spot Acton's brown Stetson among the sea of heads, when Elizabeth and Ryan raced over to meet her.

"We're sitting over here by the window," Ryan told her. "Uncle Acton is saving our table."

Elizabeth grabbed Stephanie's elbow as she stared up at the bundle in her arms. "Is that Linus? Can we see him?"

"Wait until we sit down," Ryan scolded his sister.

Elizabeth stuck her tongue out at him, but didn't argue.

Stephanie patted the girl's head. "It's okay. You can see Linus as soon as we get settled," she promised.

Grinning from ear to ear, the girl skipped ahead of them to the booth, then gestured to the side of the table where Acton was sitting.

"You can sit there, Miss Stephanie. By Uncle Acton," she said.

Before Stephanie reached the booth, Acton stood up and reached for the baby. "Here. Let me hold the little guy while you take a seat."

Acton hardly seemed like the daddy type. Yet here he was with two young children and offering to help her with the baby. *Could Dayna and the others be wrong about the man?* she wondered.

She handed the baby over to him, then slid onto

the smooth bench seat. "Thanks for your help," she told him. "And I'm sorry you had to wait so long."

"No problem." Still standing, he peeled back the blanket covering Linus's face and peered down at the baby. "Hey, he's cute as a button."

Stephanie said, "I think so, too."

Grinning, he gazed at Linus a moment longer, then gently handed him down to Stephanie.

"Okay, it's time to take orders. Who wants what?" He glanced at Stephanie and winked. "And don't be bashful. Order anything you want."

From you or the menu?

The naughty thought came out of nowhere, shocking Stephanie with its implications. She wasn't setting her eye on this handsome cowboy. Not in the least!

Thankfully, the children diverted her attention as they gave him their complicated requests. Once they were finished, Stephanie followed with her choice of a fish sandwich and fries.

Acton left to go put in their orders and Stephanie comfortably positioned Linus in the crook of her arm. Across the table, Elizabeth and Ryan leaned eagerly forward to get a closer look at the baby.

"Boy, he's really tiny," Ryan said, then wrinkled his nose. "Reckon I was ever that little?"

"Probably," Stephanie told him.

"His eyes are open," Elizabeth said. "Can he see us?"

"Yes, just not in the same way you and I can see," Stephanie explained. "He'll be able to see you better when he gets a few weeks older."

Elizabeth's head tilted curiously to one side as she regarded Stephanie. "Uncle Acton said you were a foster mother. Is that like our mother?"

The child's innocent question sent a pang of regret through Stephanie. "Not exactly. But I love and care for baby Linus just like she loves and cares for you two."

Thankfully, that explanation seemed to satisfy the girl, and before any more questions could be asked, Acton returned to their table carrying a tray laden with food.

After taking a seat next to Stephanie, he passed the food around the table and helped the kids situate their meals and drinks.

Stephanie was thinking how good he was with the children when he asked, "Would you like me to hold Linus while you eat? It's kind of hard trying to hold your food with only one hand."

"Thanks, but I'm used to it," she told him, while secretly surprised that he was being so thoughtful. Was this guy too good to be true? "I have a carrier in the car, but I prefer holding him. And he seems to like it better this way."

"Well, if you get tired just let me know," he told her.

For the next few minutes as they ate the casual

meal, the children plied her with questions about the cats and other animals that she helped treat.

Stephanie enjoyed their chatter. But it wasn't enough of a distraction to draw her attention from Acton. With his tall, lanky frame sitting only inches from her, she could practically feel the heat exuding from his body and smell the faint masculine scent emanating from the green plaid Western shirt he was wearing.

"We're finished eating, Uncle Acton," Ryan suddenly announced. "Can we go to the playground?"

Acton glanced toward the glassed-in area designated for children's play. "Okay. But be sure and watch out for your little sister. And don't be picking on any of the other kids."

Ryan looked properly insulted. "I'm not like Mikey Walters."

Acton waved the kids on and they wasted no time racing to the playground. Once they were gone, the table seemed incredibly quiet.

Acton slanted her an apologetic look. "I know they're noisy, but they're basically pretty good kids," he said.

"I think they're lovely. Do you spend much time with them?"

"Probably more than I should. Gina constantly accuses me of spoiling them. I just like to make them happy."

"So you like children? Or just your niece and nephew?"

Now why had that question come out of her mouth? She wasn't sizing him up for fatherhood, or anything close to it.

He nodded. "I've always liked kids. Probably because my brothers say I'm just a big kid myself. And I guess that's partly true. I like to have fun. But they forget that I'm a grown man now."

He was definitely that, Stephanie thought. At least, on the outside.

Linus squirmed and she glanced down to see he was chewing on his fist. "So are Elizabeth and Ryan the only niece and nephew you have?"

"My two older brothers are still single—like me." He gestured to Linus. "It's probably none of my business but how did you happen to be this little guy's foster mother?"

She pulled a bottle out of the diaper bag she'd carried with her and offered it to Linus. He latched on with a hunger that made her smile.

Glancing at Acton, she said, "I'm surprised. I thought everyone around town had heard about the baby being left at Rambling Rose Pediatric Center."

Acton's mouth fell open. "You mean Linus is *that* baby?"

"So you did hear about it?"

He nodded. "Mom was talking about the incident at dinner one evening. Anytime something happens involving a baby she gets all teary-eyed. You know how women are."

"Yes, I know," she said, finding it an effort to keep a straight face. "In case you failed to notice, I am one."

Ruddy color washed over his face. "Oh, damn. Sorry, Stephanie. I wasn't thinking. I mean, I've noticed. I've definitely noticed you're a woman."

She smiled at his flustered apology. "I couldn't help teasing you a bit," she said. "As for me fostering Linus, I just happened to be the first eligible person that was available to take him. And I'm very glad I was. He's a joy to me."

"So what about his parents? Mom said the mother ran off and can't be found?"

"That's true. After she left the baby at the pediatric center, she disappeared. How or why, no one seems to know."

"I assume the authorities are trying to locate her?" he asked.

Stephanie sighed. "Well, it's all a bit complicated. You see, there's a thing called the Safe Haven law that legally protects a parent from leaving a child at a safe house. Which, in this case, was the pediatric center. So that means they can't track her down for child abandonment. But if the mother is considered ill or in danger they can search for her."

Nodding, he said, "Sounds as though the law officials have to walk a fine line with this sort of case."

"Exactly. But so far there's been no news from anyone regarding Laurel's whereabouts."

He shook his head with dismay. "That's tough. So what now? Are you going to keep on being Linus's mother?"

Nodding, she said, "If his biological mother shows up, naturally that will end my role as Linus's foster parent. If she's never located, I'd love to legally adopt him."

"What about the dad? He has to be somewhere— unless the guy is dead."

Stephanie grimaced. "From what the mother implied, the man wasn't a part of their lives. Even so, I think there's an effort being made to find him, too. Just in case he might want to make a legal claim of Linus. But locating him might prove difficult. Laurel didn't share any valuable information about the man."

"What a loss. For both parents."

Acton obviously considered a baby to be a precious blessing, which was more than Stephanie could say for the guys she'd dated. Most of them would have bolted at the sight of a baby. Was she beginning to see a sign hanging around Acton's neck with the word *good* written on it?

"Well, for now I'm going to do my best to make sure Linus knows he's wanted," she said.

He sipped his cola, then shifted around on the

seat so that he was facing her. "I'm glad you agreed to have dinner with us, Stephanie."

"I'm glad, too." Without even trying, Acton lifted her spirits and reminded her that she needn't be serious all the time. "On weekdays my brothers often work late, so usually I'm eating alone. It's nice to have company."

"So you live with your brothers," he mused. "How does that work out for you?"

"It's good. Our house is spacious enough for me to have my own suite of rooms. Which is especially nice now that I have Linus. That way we don't disturb my brothers."

His blue eyes were studying her keenly and she figured he was thinking she led a boring life. And compared to his, it probably was.

"It's good that you have your own space. I'm just now learning what that's like."

"You don't live on your family's ranch?" she asked.

"I do live on our ranch, the Diamond D. Just not in the big ranch house. A couple of months ago I moved into my grandparents' old house. You see, Grandmother Hatti has had a few health issues. Nothing serious, but she's not quite as spry as she used to be, so my parents persuaded her to move in with them. I moved out so that she could have my room and everyone wouldn't be so crammed in."

"That was generous of you."

She watched his lips take on a guilty slant.

"Not really. I got the whole house to myself. Unless Shawn or Danny—my brothers—get the bright idea to move in with me. And I don't think that's going to happen."

"You like living on your own?"

"Most of the time. Other times I miss the hustle and bustle in the big house. And to be honest, I'm not fond of cleaning up after myself. But I try to keep things tidy."

"Who does your cooking?"

He tapped a finger against his chest. "I do all my own cooking. In fact, I'm the only one of my brothers who knows how to cook. Just to prove it, I'll fix supper for you one night. As long as you don't ask for gourmet dishes. I'm not into that kind of stuff."

Supper at his place? With no one else around? That would be a risky temptation—for her. For him it would probably be no more than having a friend over to share a meal. "I might take you up on that… someday," she told him.

Seeing Linus's mouth had gone slack around the bottle's nipple, Stephanie placed the baby on her shoulder and gently rubbed his back until he burped.

"Who does your cooking?" he asked.

Though it shouldn't have, his question caught her off guard. Mainly because she didn't like admitting that her family had Manny, the ranch's caretaker who also did most all the cooking. It bothered her to think the people of Rambling Rose might look down on the Fortune family for being so wealthy.

She said, "We have a great guy who cooks for the family. Which is a good for me. I've never been very good in the kitchen. The best I can do is a couple of Cuban dishes. That's what I liked to eat when we all lived in Fort Lauderdale. Since we moved here I've fallen in love with Tex-Mex food."

As she talked, she'd noticed the look in his eyes hadn't changed to boredom. He still appeared to be actually interested to hear about her life. The idea definitely warmed her. Most of her past boyfriends would've already turned the conversation back to themselves.

"There's nothing better," he agreed.

He plucked up a leftover fry and dipped it into a pool of ketchup. Stephanie found herself studying his hand, with its long tanned fingers. When she'd shaken hands with him the day he'd brought Seymour to the clinic, she'd felt hard calluses on his palm. Now she wondered how it would feel to have that work-worn palm rest against her cheek. To have it slide over her bare skin. To have it—

"Do you like living here in Texas? In Rambling Rose?"

The questions pulled her out of the erotic trance and she prayed he wouldn't notice the wave of heat rushing to her face.

Clearing her throat, she said, "I love it. Rambling

Rose is just the right size. Not too big or too small. And I especially like the people."

To her surprise, he reached for her hand and folded it inside his.

"I hope that means you like me, too," he said gently.

Stephanie's heart couldn't seem to decide if it wanted to skip or do a wild jig.

"I... Of course I like you," she finally said. "And your little niece and nephew, too."

His eyelids lowered while the corners of his lips curved into a sexy grin. Just looking at his face so close was causing heat to roar through her like flames in the wind.

Oh, Lord, she needed to free her hand and put some sensible space between the two of them. But how was she going to do that without looking like a prude?

Stephanie's dilemma was suddenly solved as Elizabeth and Ryan came rushing up to the table. Acton released her hand and turned his attention to the kids.

"We want ice cream, Uncle Acton," Elizabeth said. "Can we have some?"

"It's 'may' we, Lizzie, not 'can,'" Ryan corrected her as though he was an expert on grammar.

The girl crossed her arms against her chest as she sneered at her brother. "Know-it-all! You ask for the ice cream! And if we don't get it, it'll be your fault!"

With a covert wink at Stephanie, Acton said,

"There's no cause for this kind of commotion. You both ate everything you asked for, so I'm going to say yes."

He pulled out his wallet and handed a bill to Ryan. "You're in charge of the money, Ryan. But let Elizabeth order whatever she wants. The money that's left over you can split evenly between you. Okay?"

"Yeah!" Ryan exclaimed.

Elizabeth gave Acton's neck a huge hug. "Thank you, Uncle Acton!"

The two kids took off in an excited rush and Stephanie gave him a pointed smile. "I think Gina has a point about you spoiling them."

His grin was shamelessly guilty. "You're supposed to have fun when you're a kid. Come to think of it, you're supposed to have fun when you're a grown-up, too. Are you having fun yet, Stephanie?"

Without thinking, she burst out laughing. "I'm having loads of fun, Acton."

And as the sound rolled out of her, she realized it had been a long while since she'd felt this carefree. And even longer since she'd enjoyed the company of a man.

Chapter Four

The next afternoon, after the clock had passed regular school hours, Stephanie began watching for Acton and the children to show up at Paws and Claws to collect the cats. But as the closing hour neared without any sign of the three, she began to wonder if Gina had changed her mind about letting the children adopt the cats.

Which would be disappointing for two reasons. She wanted the cats to have a real home. And she wanted to see Acton again. It was that simple and that complicated.

Last night, after she and Linus had gone home, she'd spent hours thinking about the man. And today, she'd been trying to convince herself he was just a friend. The problem with that was she'd never felt like this toward a friend.

Knowing her history with men, her brothers would surely advise her to forget about Acton. A young lothario wasn't what she needed in her life. Especially now that she had Linus to consider. Yet it felt so good and right to be with him.

Pushing the swirling thoughts aside, she walked over to a large kennel where a brown-and-black shaggy dog with a cast on his leg was watching her with pleading eyes. Several days ago, the poor thing had been struck by a vehicle and a Good Samaritan had brought the injured dog to the clinic. Thankfully, Dr. Neil had managed to successfully operate on the leg and so far the dog was recovering at a rapid pace.

"Hi, Buddy," she said softly. "Ready to try for a little walk?"

Dr. Neil had prescribed the dog three short walks a day and because he'd not yet had his third excursion today, Stephanie attached a leash to the mixed breed's collar and allowed him to step out of the ground-level kennel.

Wagging his tail with excitement, Buddy, a name the clinic staff had given him, let out a happy bark and Stephanie took a moment to rub his head.

"What a champ you are," she said to the dog. "Let's walk down the hall and show everyone how good you're doing."

They left the rehab room and started down the long hallway that led to the waiting area. Along the way, Leonard, an older man who'd been a longtime assistant to Dr. Neil, stopped to give Buddy an encouraging pat. "He's going to get along fine on that leg. Are you going to adopt him, Stephanie?"

Stephanie let out a good-natured groan. "You know me, Leonard. I already have a small menagerie. But my dogs live outside and their fenced-in yard is plenty big enough to accommodate a third. And I confess—I'm getting a soft spot for Buddy."

"Hey, Stephanie, you have a visitor."

She looked around to see Dayna and Acton standing at the far end of the hallway, but his niece and nephew were nowhere in sight.

"Excuse me, Leonard, I need to speak with this person."

Leonard peered down the hallway. "That's Acton Donovan," he stated.

"You know him?" she asked.

"Been friends with his family for many years. Fine folks. They raise some of the best Brangus cattle around these parts. Tell him I said hello. I better run. Dr. Neil is waiting on me."

Leonard hurried away and Stephanie urged Buddy forward. By the time she reached Acton, her heart was pounding and not from the exertion of the walk.

She didn't understand why, but seeing the man again was like looking at blue sky after a rainstorm.

"Hello, Acton."

"Hi, Stephanie. Sorry I'm running late."

They were smiling at each other, a fact that Dayna was clearly taking note of.

"No problem," she assured him, then asked, "Didn't Elizabeth and Ryan come with you?"

He shook his head. "They both forgot they had after-school projects this evening. They made me promise to pick up the cats for them. I've already filled out the necessary papers and paid the fees."

"I'm happy for the cats. But I'm disappointed that Elizabeth and Ryan couldn't be here. I was looking forward to seeing them again," she said.

He chuckled. "After putting up with those two last night, I'm surprised. They can wear on a body's nerves."

Picking up on his comment, Dayna cast a shrewd gaze from Stephanie to Acton. "Last night? What happened with the kids last night?"

"Just a hamburger, that's all," he said.

That's all it had probably been to him, Stephanie thought dismally. To her it had been a special evening. It had given her the opportunity to see Acton in a totally different light than the one Dayna and the other female staffers put him in.

Thankfully, the other woman turned her attention to Buddy, who was standing obediently at Stephanie's side.

"Look at you, Buddy. You hardly have a limp now.

Next thing we know you'll have that cast off and be chasing squirrels."

Stephanie explained to Acton how Buddy had wound up at the clinic and ended it with Leonard's idea that she adopt the dog when he was well enough to go home.

"I really think you ought to take him, Acton," she suggested. "It would be good for Seymour to have a friend."

The suggestion caused him to laugh. "Seymour have a friend? He'd try to tear Buddy's head off!"

"Poor Seymour. You're underestimating your dog," Stephanie told him.

Acton laughed again. "Listen, I made the mistake of letting Seymour watch *Lassie* reruns. Now he thinks he's just as good an actor as that famous collie. All the nice behavior he shows you is just a big performance. He's actually Cujo in disguise."

Stephanie couldn't stop a giggle. "Oh, stop it, Acton! That's horrible!"

"Horrible is right. I can't turn my back on the monster," he said, then added with a mischievous wink, "Only kidding. Seymour is a loyal mutt. Most of the time."

Sobering her laughter, Stephanie said, "If you're ready to collect the cats, I'll help you. But I need to finish Buddy's walk first."

Dayna promptly reached for Buddy's leash. "You

two go on," she said coyly. "I'll be happy to take Buddy on the rest of his walk."

Dayna and the dog turned and headed back down the hallway. Stephanie cast Acton an apologetic look.

"I apologize for Dayna's little insinuations. She has this silly idea that you like me."

"What's silly about that? I do like you."

Clasping her hands in front of her, Stephanie let out a long sigh. "Dayna means a different kind of like. And it's embarrassing. So please just ignore her."

His eyebrows arched upward until they very nearly disappeared beneath the brim of his hat. "It's embarrassing for you to be associated with me?"

"No! That's not what I meant. I was afraid all her sly innuendoes were embarrassing you."

Clearly amused, he said, "I'm twenty-five years old, Stephanie. I suppose by most standards that's young. But I'm past the age of being easily embarrassed. And for your information, I'm feeling rather flattered that she's linking you to me."

Stephanie decided she should've never started this conversation. The more he talked, the worse it got.

"I'm glad you feel that way," she told him, while trying not to melt with pleasure at his compliment. She'd be a fool to let herself swoon over a man who had the reputation of being a cowboy Casanova.

"Well, that's that," he said a few minutes later as he shut the back door of the truck. In the carriers that were safely positioned on the floorboard, the two cats were howling in protest.

"You're probably going to hear plenty of meowing the whole trip," she warned. "But they'll quiet down once you get them to your sister's place."

Acton rubbed his palms down the thighs of his jeans and wondered why he was suddenly feeling nervous. He'd never felt anxious about asking a woman to spend time with him. Stephanie shouldn't be any different. But she was different, he realized. Not because she was a sister to the high-rolling Fortune brothers. But because she was sweet and sincere and being around her made him feel good.

Did that mean he was falling in love with her? Acton didn't know. He'd never been in love before. But he did know that the warmth she evoked in him was like nothing he'd ever felt before.

Rubbing her hands up and down her arms to ward off the chill of the February wind, she said, "Well, I'd better get back inside."

"Before you do that I, uh, was wondering if you'd mind riding over to Gina's house with me? To get the cats settled in," he explained. "I won't mind waiting out here until you get off work."

Her lips parted with surprise and Acton found himself staring at them, imagining how they would feel against his.

"Oh, I don't know, Acton," she said in a doubtful tone. "Linus is at day care and—"

"I won't keep you that long. Promise." He used his forefinger to make an *X* across his chest. "I'd really like for you to meet my sister. The kids have been telling her all about you. I think she's getting the idea that you're some sort of princess."

She let out a little laugh and Acton felt something deep inside him go as soft as pudding. He couldn't deny it was a joy to hear her laughter and see her smile. She needed to do it more, he thought. With him.

"Your sister is definitely in for a surprise," she said.

"Then you'll go with me?" he asked.

As she considered his invitation, Acton watched her wrestle with the long strands of hair being whipped about by the wind. Today she was wearing a pair of dark jeans and a canary-yellow blouse that buttoned down the front. The bright color made her red hair stand out even more.

From the time he'd entered his teens, Acton had taken extra notice of pretty girls, and down through the years, he'd ogled plenty of them. But he'd never stopped to appreciate all the tiny things that made them attractive. With Stephanie, every minute detail caught his attention. What did that mean?

"I suppose I could go," she finally answered. "But I can only stay for a few minutes. I don't want to leave Linus at the day care any longer than necessary."

"That's fine. That's okay," he said happily, then gestured behind her to the building. "You go on and finish your work. I'll wait for you out here with the cats."

She glanced at her watch. "Give me ten minutes."

As she hurried back into the clinic, Acton realized he'd give her all night, just to spend five minutes alone with her.

Oh, brother, he was sicker than a calf at weaning time, he thought. And if he didn't man up soon and get over this constant urge to be with Stephanie, he was going to end up being some kind of whimpering sap.

Acton's sister, Gina, lived in a rambling redbrick house on the north edge of town. The yard was perfectly landscaped with shrubs and rose bushes, while most of the house was shaded by the huge, spreading limbs of a live oak tree.

"This is nice," Stephanie said as he pulled to a stop in the driveway behind a white family-type SUV. "And the roses growing near the house are blooming like it's the middle of June instead of February."

"I guess from living in Florida you're used to a mild climate," he said.

She nodded. "I am. Before we moved here to Texas I thought I'd be moving into cold, snowy winters. I had all these plans to buy furry coats and dress boots. Then I find out the temperature hardly dips low enough to cause a frost. So I ended up not buying any heavy clothing."

"Sometimes the weather surprises us with sleet or freezing drizzle," he said. "But let's not hope for that. During those storms it takes a heck of a lot of work to make sure the baby calves have enough shelter."

Stephanie glanced over at him. He was such a laid-back, fun guy that sometimes she forgot he worked the serious job of ranching. She didn't know all that much about raising cattle, but enough to know that taking care of large herds of cows and calves couldn't be easy.

He parked the truck, then helped her step to the ground. After they'd collected the cats from the back, they walked to the concrete porch that ran halfway across the front of the house.

Acton rang the doorbell, and within a few seconds, the door opened and Stephanie found herself looking at an older, female version of Acton. The tall blonde with shoulder-length hair and bright blue eyes smiled warmly at her.

"Hello," she said.

Acton wasted no time in stepping up and wrapping a hand around Stephanie's arm, as though she belonged to him. The thought left her feeling ridiculously feminine and even a bit cherished.

"This is Stephanie Fortune, sis. She kindly offered to help me deliver the cats to you. She's an animal expert so you can ask her anything about taking care of them."

Smiling, Gina pushed the door wider and made a sweeping gesture with her arm to usher them inside.

"An expert? Wow! For Acton to put you on that kind of pedestal you must be good."

Stephanie waved off the woman's compliment as they entered. "I'm hardly an expert. But I have worked as a vet assistant for the past six years. After that length of time you do learn a bit."

"I'm sure you've learned more than a bit," Gina said. She paused in the middle of a large, comfortable living room, then clasped her hands out in front of her. "So should I simply let the cats loose here? The other cat we had—Tinker—was very frightened when we first brought him home. It took days to get him to come out from under the bed."

Stephanie nodded. "That's not unusual. But maybe we can do something to help these two get acquainted more easily. Do you have a small room you can shut off? One without too many things they can hide under?"

Gina thought for a moment. "The mudroom. There's nothing in there except the washer and dryer, a set of sinks and a dirty-clothes hampers."

"That sounds perfect," Stephanie said. "Cats feel more comfortable in a small space and they'll be more likely to let Ryan and Elizabeth come near them. Once they get fully acquainted with you and the kids, you can let them have free rein of the house."

Acton shot his sister a confident grin. "See, I told you she was an expert."

There was a note of pride in Acton's compliment and it touched Stephanie in a way that took her by surprise.

Jeff, one of the first guys she'd dated in college, had thought her job as a veterinarian assistant was little more than cleaning cages and litter boxes. When she'd tried to explain that she actually helped treat the animals, he'd laughed as though she couldn't possibly be smart enough for such a job. In the end, she'd shown Jeff exactly how smart she was by dumping him.

On the other hand, Acton was often praising her, and though most of what he said was probably little more than mild flirtation, she felt he was being genuine when he talked about her experience with animal care.

Gina gave her brother a calculating look. "Yes, I can see. She's smarter than you are."

Acton groaned. "Oh, sis, don't go telling stuff on me. I'm already having a hard enough time trying to make Stephanie like me."

With a shake of her head, Gina smiled pointedly at Stephanie. "Don't believe a word this guy tells you. It's all lies."

Acton glared at her. "Gina! You're breaking my

heart. Just see if I help you paint that damned garage again!"

Laughing, Gina hooked an arm affectionately through Acton's and tugged him toward an open doorway. "Come on, baby brother, I'm only teasing. Let's take care of these cats and then you and Stephanie might like some coffee and cookies. I just took them out of the oven."

A few minutes later, after Stephanie helped Gina set up makeshift beds and litter boxes, and the cats were exploring their new digs, they all returned to the kitchen.

"Sit at the bar or the table. Any place you like," Gina told Stephanie. "Make yourself at home. Acton always does."

"Thank you," Stephanie told her. "I can only stay a few minutes. I have to pick up my baby at day care."

At a white farm table, Acton pulled out a chair for Stephanie, then sat next to her.

Gina carried two cups of coffee over to the table. "Acton told me that you were fostering the abandoned baby. I admire you, Stephanie. Especially since the whole situation is uncertain at best."

After taking a careful sip, she said, "No matter what's going on with his parents, Linus needs to be mothered. To be honest, I hope his real mother is alive."

"So sad to think of any mother leaving her baby

behind. I can't remember anything like this ever happening in Rambling Rose."

She placed a plate of cookies in front of Stephanie and Acton, then took a seat at the end of the table.

"Is Jack still at work?" Acton asked as he reached for a snickerdoodle.

Gina explained to Stephanie. "Jack is my husband. He works for a heating-and-cooling company."

"And repairs appliances on the side," Acton added.

"Jack was called to the high school gymnasium. There's a basketball game tonight and the heat in the locker rooms went on the blink. He'll probably show up about the time I have to leave to pick up the kids. Hopefully, he won't let the cats out. I'd better send him a text and warn him before he gets here."

"That's not a bad idea, sis."

Gina leaned back in her chair and eyed Stephanie with open curiosity. "So the Fortunes who've been building the fancy things around town are your brothers? I work as a secretary for a real estate agent so I hear if a new roof goes on a barn. Your brothers have already made a huge mark in Rambling Rose."

Nodding, Stephanie said, "My brothers dream big. And they want to build big things for Rambling Rose. I realize not everyone around here is happy with what they're planning, but they truly want what's good for the town."

Gina's smile held more understanding than Stephanie expected.

"Change of any kind always makes waves," she reasoned. "You shouldn't worry. These things have a way of working out."

"I hope you're right."

Gina said, "Until Acton told me about you, I didn't realize the Fortune brothers had a sister."

Stephanie was surprised that he'd mentioned her to his sister. She'd certainly not brought up the subject of Acton to her brothers. Only because she couldn't say the word *man* without all three of them going into long lectures about getting her heart broken for the umpteenth time. She wasn't keen on being reminded that she was a loser in the romance department.

She said, "Callum, Steven and Dillon are my brothers who make up Fortune Brothers Construction. And there's Wiley, another brother, still living back in Florida. I also have triplet sisters, Ashley, Megan and Nicole. They're still in Fort Lauderdale, also, but I think they're strongly considering moving here to Rambling Rose."

"You're from a big family," Gina remarked. "And triplet sisters—that's amazing! I can't imagine dealing with three at once. Ryan and Elizabeth are two years apart and they're a handful. Just ask Acton."

Stephanie looked at him and smiled. "I think he handles them quite well."

Acton smiled back at her and suddenly some sort of invisible force arced between them. Except for the two of them, everything in the room seemed to fade away.

If it hadn't been for Gina clearing her throat and disrupting the moment, Stephanie would've continued to stare at Acton like a moonstruck fool. Instead, she managed to shake away the dazed feeling and turn her attention back to the other woman when she asked a question.

"Are your sisters anything like you?"

"Not really," Stephanie answered. "They're four years younger than me and have a totally different mind-set. And they're much prettier."

"That couldn't be possible," Acton said.

Blushing now, Stephanie shook her head. "Has your brother always blurted out this kind of thing?"

Gina laughed and the sound reminded her of Acton's laughter. It was an easy, happy sound and Stephanie had no doubt the Donovan home had always been a warm and loving place.

"As long as I can remember he's been this way. Grandma Hatti calls him the charmer of the family. Though, I have a few other choice names for him," she teased. "With Acton being the baby of the family, he's always gotten away with murder."

Acton feigned an innocent look. "What can I say? I didn't tell my parents to quit having kids after me."

Gina said, "I'll be honest, Stephanie—most of my friends are curious about what that mansion you call home looks like on the inside. We're Texans and we've seen lavish before, but not here in Rambling Rose."

Stephanie shrugged. "It is luxurious. But to be honest, I don't need that much space. And I'm not a fancy person. But my brothers wanted the place and they convinced me to go along with them. The part I like about it is that I have plenty of room for my pets. Two dogs and two cats and a rabbit."

"And she's going to adopt another dog with a cast on his leg," Acton added.

"You have more energy and patience than I do," Gina said with a laugh.

On a nearby counter, Gina's cell phone pinged and she left the table to check it.

"That's probably the kids texting to let me know they're ready to be picked up. Just wait until you have older children, Stephanie. Most of the time, you'll feel like a taxi driver."

Stephanie rose from the chair and carried her cup over to the sink. "It was very nice meeting you, Gina. Let me know if you have any problems with the cats. I'll be glad to help."

Gina reached over and gave her a brief hug. "I hope we can be friends, Stephanie."

"I'd love that," she told her. "Perhaps you could bring the kids out sometime and let them play with my cats and dogs? I'll show you my part of the house."

"Now that's an invitation I won't let you forget," Gina promised.

They told Acton's sister goodbye and once they were in his truck, headed back to Paws and Claws, Acton surprised her by bringing up the subject of Gina visiting the Fame and Fortune Ranch.

"That was nice of you to invite my sister out to your place. We've never really brushed shoulders with anyone like you, Stephanie. She'll enjoy seeing how you live."

From the corner of her eye, she studied Acton's profile. Did he really see her as someone that different from him? The thought hurt her. One of the things that had drawn her to him in the first place was the fact that he hadn't made a big issue of her being a Fortune, or having money. But now she wondered if he was actually like all the other guys she'd known—eyeing her as a dollar sign instead of a woman with normal wants and needs.

"Yes, I live in a fancy house. But that doesn't make me different, Acton. I live just like other women my age in Rambling Rose."

He arched his eyebrows in question and glanced at her. "What is your age?"

"Hasn't anyone told you that it's a no-no to ask a woman her age?"

Amusement crinkled the corners of his eyes and mouth. "My dad warned me a time or two, but I don't always follow his advice."

That was hardly a surprise. Everything about him shouted rebel.

She said, "I've hardly reached the point of being ashamed to reveal my age. I'm twenty-seven."

"Well, to be frank, Stephanie, I don't know of any twenty-seven-year-old women who live as you do. You've already told me the ranch caretaker also does the family cooking. I'll bet you have house-keepers, too."

He made it sound like having hired help was a crime. "That's right. We have people to come in and help with the cleaning. And a groundskeeper, along with a man to care for the horses and stables. But none of that means I'm a spoiled girl. That is what you're getting at, isn't it?"

His laugh was a sound of disbelief rather than one of humor. "*Spoiled* is the last word I'd use to describe you, Stephanie. I can see you work hard. And just so you know, I'm not looking to be your friend because you have money."

Stephanie had heard that before. Not in those exact words, but close. And for years, she'd chosen to believe them. Every woman needed to be wanted just for being herself. But after a few humiliating attempts at romance, she'd learned how naive it was to blindly trust a man. Men were out to get whatever they could from her. Both physically and monetarily. Yet in spite of those hard lessons, she desperately wanted to believe Acton was different from the jerks who'd strolled in and out of her life.

Deciding it would be best to keep things light between them, she teased, "No, you're looking to be my friend because you think I'm an expert with animals—especially a dog named Seymour."

He laughed. "How did you ever guess that was my ulterior motive?"

By now they had reached the Paws and Claws parking lot. Acton braked the truck to a stop next to Stephanie's car, then surprised her by reaching across the console for her hand.

As his fingers wrapped around hers, there was a glint in his eyes that gave her the impression he was going to lift the back of her hand to his lips.

The idea caused the breath of air she was trying to draw in to lodge in her throat, but she did her best not to cough or sputter. No matter if she fell over in a dead faint, she thought—that would be better than letting him know he'd thrown her senses into a major earthquake.

"I saw a flyer on the bulletin board in the waiting room about a Valentine's fund-raiser for Paws and Claws this coming Friday. Are you going to be helping with the event?"

Caught off guard by the unexpected question, she stared blankly at him. "The fund-raiser? Oh, uh, yes, the whole Paws and Claws staff will be contributing in some way. It's going to take place downtown in The Shoppes—that's the old Woolworth's building my brothers just finished restructuring. Dr. Neil hopes the function will raise a ton of money to offset caring for stray and orphaned animals. Why do you ask?"

Even as she spoke, all her attention was on her hand in his. If he continued to hold her hand, it was going to combust into flames, she thought wildly. The heat from his fingers was racing up her arm and, she feared, straight to her face.

A lopsided grin curved his lips. "It's a good cause. I thought I might volunteer to help. If that's okay with you."

His thumb began to move gently against the back of her hand and Stephanie felt goose bumps erupt over her forearms. How could the simple touch of his hand make her feel hot and cold at the same time? It was downright scary.

Forcing herself to breathe, she said, "You don't need my permission to volunteer. All help is welcome."

His fingers tightened around hers, and though she couldn't be sure, she thought his face was a fraction closer to hers than it had been a moment ago.

He said, "I don't want to make you feel awkward."

Puzzled, she asked, "Why would I feel awkward?"

He shrugged. "Well, Dayna already thinks the two of us are a couple. And I can see that bothers you."

It bothered her because they weren't a couple.

And they had no business trying to be, she thought gloomily. She wasn't his type and he was…well, he'd be another heartbreak for her.

"What Dayna or anyone else thinks hardly matters," she said. "As long as it doesn't bother you, then it doesn't bother me."

A wide smile exposed a set of beautiful white teeth and Stephanie found herself wondering how it might feel to have them gently nipping her skin, her lips. He'd be a generous, giving lover. Somehow she knew that.

"I'm glad you feel that way, Stephanie. So I'll be around to help. Just send me a text to let me know when the work starts."

"I don't have your number."

"Yes, you do. It's on Seymour's chart."

Seymour. That dog had put her life into upheaval, she thought.

"Okay. I'll text you."

She eased her hand from his and turned to climb out of the truck, but he caught her by the shoulder and gently urged her back around.

"Not so fast," he said gently. "Before you go I want to thank you."

Before Stephanie could guess his intentions, he leaned forward and pressed a kiss to her cheek.

Her heart pounding, she stared wondrously at him. "What are you thanking me for?"

The smile on his face disappeared and for the

first time since she'd met him, a serious expression took its place.

"Just for being you, Stephanie."

Without even trying, he made her feel special. But common sense told her she couldn't take him seriously. He'd only end up breaking her heart.

A lump in her throat, she pulled her hand from his and scurried out of the truck before he could notice her eyes were filled with tears.

Chapter Five

Stephanie was sitting on the couch, changing Linus's diaper, when the door opened and Becky stuck her head inside.

"Knock, knock. Can you stand a bit of company?" she asked.

Happy to see Callum's wife, she motioned for her sister-in-law to join her. "Come in, Becky. I'd love company."

The pretty brunette entered the suite and walked over to the couch, where Linus was lying on his back, kicking his arms and legs as Stephanie fastened the disposable diaper in place.

She said, "He's definitely grown since I saw him

a few days ago. Aww, and look at those eyes, they're sparkling. What a cutie!"

Stephanie tugged the navy blue onesie back in place and snapped it together. "I'll let you watch him, while I go dispose of his dirty diaper," she told Becky. "He's too young to roll over yet. But you never know."

"Sure. I'll be glad to keep an eye on the little man."

Stephanie carried the diaper to an airtight plastic container in the bathroom, then returned to the living area, where Becky had taken a seat on the cushion next to Linus.

"I took him in for a checkup today," she told Becky. "Dr. Green said he's healthy. Thank God for that. By the way, I didn't see you there. Were you not working this afternoon?"

"I was. I must've been on my lunch break."

Stephanie nodded as she sat in an armchair. "Probably so. I had the appointment scheduled on my lunch hour so I wouldn't miss work."

"You have a fire in the fireplace tonight," Becky noted. "It feels great."

Stephanie followed Becky's gaze over to a small fireplace that stretched across one corner of the room. Her cats, Violet and Daisy, were stretched out near the hearth, while Orville sat observing the flames from a safer distance.

"I'll be so happy when this wintery weather

moves out," Becky remarked. "I've been bundling up the twins and keeping my fingers crossed that they don't catch cold."

"Where are the twins? Don't tell me Callum is chasing after them."

Becky laughed. "Actually, he is. When I left them in the den, he had both girls in his lap and was attempting to read them a story about a horned toad and a dragonfly. If that last more than five minutes, I'll be surprised."

Stephanie chuckled. "It still surprises me to see Callum putting himself in daddy mode."

Sighing, Becky covered Linus with a light blanket. "To be honest, I still have a hard time believing he really wanted me and the girls as his ready-made family."

"Callum loves you and the twins more than anything," Stephanie assured her. "But my little ready-made family?" She nodded at Linus. "Well, that's a shaky matter."

Becky's expression was empathetic. "I guess it would be pointless to tell you not to worry."

Stephanie sighed. "Linus might be the closest thing I'll ever have to having a child of my own."

Becky groaned. "Stephanie! You make it sound like you're going to be a spinster."

"I'm sure Callum has told you stories about some of the men in my life," she said bitterly. "I've picked some real losers. Actually, I've given up on picking.

I've decided the best choice for me is to forget about a husband and try to adopt as a single mother."

Shaking her head, Becky said, "Callum explained that's why you were already eligible to be a foster mother for Linus. You'd already had a background check done in order to adopt."

"I realize that shocked them. I hadn't mentioned it before because...well, it's such a private decision and I thought they would disapprove."

"Honestly, I don't think any of them disapprove of you adopting a child. But they do frown on this idea of yours to remain single."

Stephanie snorted. "That's very funny. Anytime I mention dating someone, all I hear is discouragement."

"They believe you deserve real love. That's what they want for you."

Love. Ever since Acton had walked into Paws and Claws with Seymour trotting along beside him, she'd thought far too much about that one particular emotion.

"Actually, Becky, I have met someone that makes me think about things like love and babies and even marriage. But he's all wrong for me. So I'm trying hard not to think about him—and everything that I'm missing."

Becky suddenly scooted to the edge of her seat. "Who is this guy? If he's making you dream about love and marriage, then he can't be all wrong."

"Oh yes, he can," she said glumly. "Among other things, he's two years younger than me. How can I take a twenty-five year old man seriously?"

"So? That's just a number. I've known twenty-five-year-old men who were more mature than forty-year-olds."

"Perhaps. But he's good-looking. Too good-looking, if you know what I mean. Women go gaga over him and rightly so. Trouble is, I think he enjoys the attention. From what I hear he's dated plenty of them."

"A playboy, huh?" She shook her head. "What's his name? I might know him."

Stephanie should've never started this conversation, but Becky was the closest thing to a sister she had here in Rambling Rose. As for her triplet sisters back in Florida, Ashley, Megan and Nicole had never understood Stephanie's reluctance to jump into the dating scene with both feet. No big deal that she'd had a few bummers, they often told her. Unless she kept trying, she'd never find a good man.

When Becky asked the identity of her mystery man again, Stephanie knew there was no getting around it. "Acton Donovan," she replied. "I think his family owns and operates the Diamond D Ranch."

Becky's lips formed an *O.* "The Donovans. Sure, I know them. Gina brings her children into the pediatric center. I can't say that I've ever had any personal dealings with the men of the family. Although, I've seen them around town. They're all good-looking. And all still single, I think. I heard one of the nurses I work with say she'd like to date Acton, but as far as I know that never happened."

"From what I hear, there are plenty of women around town who'd like to date Acton. And the last thing I want to do is stand in line."

Frowning, Becky left the couch and walked over to the fireplace. "Have you actually met Acton?"

What would Becky think if she told her that the man had kissed her on the cheek yesterday? Warn her that she was playing with fire? "We've had a few meetings at the clinic. He's flirty, but fun and nice. He's offered to help with the fund-raiser Friday night."

Glancing over her shoulder, Becky smiled at Stephanie. "If that's the case, he can't be all bad. Do you think he's interested in you?"

Linus began to whimper and Stephanie went over to the couch to pick up the baby. As she positioned him against her shoulder, she said, "The girls on the staff have the idea that he likes me. I find that hard to believe. I mean, yes, I think he likes me—as in like as a friend. But I'm fairly vanilla, Becky. This guy can have rocky road…if he wants it."

Chuckling, she said, "Don't sell yourself short, Steph. Vanilla might be his favorite flavor."

She walked over to the couch and reached her arms out toward Linus. "Let me hold the little guy.

With the twins being toddlers I've almost forgotten how tiny they were at Linus's age."

Stephanie handed the baby over to her, while thinking Becky was one of the strongest, most resilient women she'd ever known. Shortly after she'd learned she was pregnant, her husband had been killed in a car accident. Since then, she'd raised the two babies alone. Until she'd met Callum and they'd fallen in love and married a few short weeks ago. Now Callum was the twins' father and loving every minute of it.

With Linus in her arms, Becky sank into the rocker and used her toe to push the chair into motion. While she rocked the baby, Stephanie walked over to a large plate glass window that overlooked the back portion of the property.

The Fame and Fortune Ranch was equipped with a huge swimming pool and a stable full of gentle riding horses, plus many other amenities that made life easy and pleasurable. It was a home that most people could only dream about, and because of this lavish place, Acton seemed to think she had everything she could possibly want. But she didn't have any of things she'd always truly wanted. Like the love of a man, or children to nurture and call her own.

She looked over at Becky. "You never did give me your opinion about Acton Donovan," Stephanie said. "Do you think he'd be trouble?"

"Aren't all men trouble?" She laughed before her

expression turned serious. "Just remember, Steph, I thought my chance for happiness was gone and I believed Callum was all wrong for me. Now look. We're married and very much in love. Anything can happen, even when it looks impossible. So I'm saying you'd be foolish to rule out Acton. Not before you give him a chance."

Acton might not want a chance with her, Stephanie thought.

And if he did? Was she brave enough to open her heart to him?

Acton spent the whole day helping his father and Shawn tag and vaccinate calves. The job was time-consuming, not to mention exhausting, and by the time they called it quits, it was too late to drive into town and see Stephanie at Paws and Claws.

Which was probably a good thing, Acton decided, as he drove the bumpy pasture road that led back to his house. If he didn't quit showing up at the animal clinic, Stephanie was going to start wondering what his intentions toward her really were, and Acton wasn't sure he could truthfully give her, or himself, the answer to that question.

Yes, he enjoyed being with her, especially two days ago when he'd picked up the cats. Everything about her turned him on. But the more he was learning about Stephanie Fortune, the more he worried that Shawn was right about her being out of his league. In the end, what could Acton really offer her?

The idea of her moving out of that palatial mansion and into his old two-story house, with its linoleum floors and wooden screen doors, was laughable. No woman in her right mind would sacrifice all that just for him. And Acton would do well to remember that.

Five minutes later, he reached the modest, white-clapboard house he called home. Seymour was waiting as Acton parked the truck beneath a live oak. The dog followed him onto a screened-in back porch, then into the kitchen.

Inside, the dog walked straight to his feed bowl and stared impatiently at Acton.

He stripped off his dusty chaps and denim jacket, then tossed them across the back of a chair. "Look, Seymour, one of us has to do some work around here. And I don't punch a time clock, so get over it."

The dog let out a single, demanding bark.

With a shake of his head, Acton went over to a corner pantry, where Seymour's food was stored.

"And you're not getting canned food tonight," he told the dog. "You ate it all and I'm not driving into town for more. Besides, the dry stuff will be better for your waistline. I'm surprised Stephanie didn't say you were fat!"

The dog whined and Acton stared at him in dismay. Surely the canine didn't know he was talking about the vet assistant who'd made his itching go away. Seymour was smart, but he wasn't human.

Acton poured a full bowl of food and was about to search the refrigerator for something to feed himself when the cell phone in his pocket dinged with a message.

Expecting it to be Shawn or Danny, he was surprised to discover the text message was from an unknown number.

Would you like to help me with a little baking this evening at my place? I'm making cookies and cupcakes for the fund-raiser.

Stephanie was inviting him to her house? He'd never expected anything like this!

Acton rapidly typed in a one-word message. When?

Whenever you can get here. I'll watch for you.

He replied that he'd be there shortly, then tossed the phone onto the cabinet counter and stomped a jig in the middle of the kitchen.

"Oowwee! Seymour, this is the best day of my life!"

Clearly unimpressed, the dog looked at him.

"Well, the second-best day," Acton told him. "I

keep forgetting the very best day was when I got you, old buddy. Just don't tell Stephanie I said so."

He raced out of the kitchen and straight down the hallway to the bathroom. As he stripped off the rest of his work clothes and stepped into the shower, he thought how shocked Shawn would be when he heard Stephanie had invited Acton to the Fame and Fortune Ranch.

But not clearly not as shocked as he was.

With Linus cradled in her arms, Stephanie met Acton at the front entrance to the house and guided him back to the main kitchen she shared with her three brothers.

"I'm surprised you agreed to this, Acton. Like I told you before, I know very little about cooking or baking. And Manny, our cook, is off tonight." She gestured to an array of ingredients and mixing bowls she'd laid out on a large work island in the middle of the room. "Do you think you can help me figure all this out?" she asked, letting her eyes look at him squarely for the first time tonight.

Dressed in faded jeans and a dark green shirt that contrasted with his light-colored hair, he was far more tempting than any cookie or cupcake they might make.

"I think I can," he told her. "After I get used to feeling like I've stepped into a palace. This place is incredible, Stephanie." He didn't bother to hide his amazement as he turned in a full circle, staring in awe at the endless rows of cabinets, tall, beamed ceilings, rich tiled floor and the most up-to-date appliances on the market. "Seymour wouldn't know what to do in this kitchen. When I left, he'd finished his supper and was lying on a braided rug in front of the gas range. This room would probably scare him."

Laughing, Stephanie carefully placed Linus in a padded carrier sitting at one end of the work island. As she fastened a safety belt across his middle, she said, "It's just a kitchen to me. I'll show you my part of the house later if you'd like—after we get the treats for the fund-raiser baked."

He continued to glance around as though he still couldn't believe what he was seeing. "I'd like that. Except I can't tell Gina. She'll be jealous that I got to visit this place before she did. Are you and Linus the only ones here?"

"No. Callum and his wife, Becky, and their one-year-old twin girls are in their section of the house. Steven, my oldest brother, usually works late with his construction crew, so I don't know if he's home yet. Dillon is in his office. I should say the office he uses here in his part of the house," she explained. "He spends most of his time on the phone conferring with the triplets on a design for the restaurant that they're planning in Rambling Rose."

He looked at her with faint surprise. "Rambling Rose is getting a new restaurant? If it's anything like this kitchen, I'm not sure the regular folks around town can afford to eat there."

Stephanie shrugged. "I purposely stay out of their business. Because it's a polarizing subject to the townspeople. If I made a point of openly siding with my brothers, some people might choose not to use Dr. Neil just because I work there."

He said, "In other words you prefer to remain neutral."

"Exactly."

He leaned over her shoulder to peer at Linus, and Stephanie breathed in the clean scent of his after-shave. If she turned slightly, her lips would almost be level with his and all she would need to do was lean in… But the man wasn't here for kissing, she told herself crossly. He was here for baking.

"Hey, Linus. When are you going to get big enough to eat a cookie?" he asked in a soft voice. "Do you even have a tooth yet?"

The gentle way he interacted with Linus never failed to surprise Stephanie. It also endeared him to her as nothing else could. "He doesn't have a tooth yet," she told him. "Maybe in another couple of months."

"He sure is cute. I've never seen him cry. Does he cry often?"

"Rarely. He's a happy baby."

He shook his head. "Ryan squalled all the time.

And Elizabeth yelled. I don't know how Gina came out of their baby years with any sense left."

He moved away and as Stephanie tried to regain her breath, she reached for a white bib apron. While she tied it on over her long dress printed with green and red flowers, he said, "I was surprised you invited me here tonight."

She glanced up at him and hoped he couldn't read the emotions she was feeling at seeing him again. Joy was pouring through her and curving the corners of her lips into a permanent smile. "I think I surprised myself by asking you over."

He smiled back at her. "I'm glad you did. And, by the way, you look very pretty. I've never seen you in a dress before or with your hair pinned up like that. The only thing you need is a magnolia in your hair and then you'd look like a tropical goddess."

Blushing, she said, "How do you know what a tropical goddess looks like?"

"Oh, I've squired plenty of them around Rambling Rose," he joked.

"I'll just bet." She laughed, then gestured to the work island. "What do you say we get to work and start with the cookies?"

"Sounds like a plan to me."

For the next few minutes, Stephanie read off the cookie recipe while Acton measured the ingredients into a large mixing bowl.

After he'd stirred everything together to make a

stiff dough, Stephanie read the next step. "Chill the dough at least an hour before rolling and cutting."

"Rolling and cutting? I've never rolled and cut," he said with a shake of his head. "I thought you spooned it onto a metal sheet and baked it."

"Well, I've never done this before," she admitted. "So I don't know what will happen if we skip that step. But I don't really have time to wait for the dough to chill. Let's do it your way. If they don't turn out, I'll cheat and go by the bakery. If I do, Sheri and Dayna will never quit teasing me, but that's okay."

He chuckled. "So you're not going to admit to them that I made these cookies?"

"Um, no. I'd never hear the end of it. For a lot of reasons."

A few minutes later, Stephanie was placing the freshly baked cookies onto a cooling rack and Acton was reading over the cupcake instructions, when her three brothers sauntered into the kitchen.

Deep in conversation, they didn't notice Acton and Stephanie at the work island. When they did finally spot them, they stopped in their tracks and stared at Acton as though he'd just stepped off a UFO.

"Stephanie! You're baking?" Steven asked.

The shock on her brothers' faces was almost comical.

"With a little help," she admitted. Then she took Acton by the arm and urged him toward the three men.

"Acton, these are my brothers. The tall dark-haired one on the left is Callum. The one in the middle, who thinks I'm a disaster in the kitchen, is Steven. And on the right with the sandy blond hair, that's Dillon. Most of the time he's the quiet one of the three."

Acton politely shook hands with each man. "It's nice to meet you all," he said.

Callum's skeptical gaze vacillated between his sister and Acton. "It's nice to meet you, too, Acton. We hope."

Hope? Oh, Lord, Stephanie thought, this curt attitude from her brothers was the last thing she needed right now.

"Stephanie hasn't mentioned you before. Are you a new boyfriend or something?"

The question came from Steven, who as the oldest of the siblings, had always considered himself the boss. He was frowning with disapproval. Which was ridiculous, Stephanie thought. He didn't know Acton. And he certainly shouldn't be judging him by his appearance.

"You're jumping to conclusions, Steven. Acton is just a friend. You don't need to start interrogating him."

She glanced at Acton and was suddenly struck by a wounded look in his eyes. Had her brothers' attitude offended him? Or had her comment about him being just a friend put the shadows in his eyes? Either way, she felt sick and helpless at the same time.

"I don't think Acton is someone we need worry about," Dillon said bluntly.

"Worry?" Acton repeated blankly as he studied the three men. "I don't get this."

"You'd get it if you knew all the losers that Stephanie has dated," Steven told him. "None of whom deserved our beautiful little sister. So just make sure you don't give us something to worry about."

"Steven!" she practically shouted at him. "I don't need this or deserve it! And neither does Acton! I'd appreciate it if all three of you would please get out of here and leave us alone."

His face grim, Steven walked out of the kitchen with Dillon following after him.

Pausing, Callum said, "We're just trying to protect you, Stephanie. That's all. We don't have anything against Acton."

"No," she drawled with sarcasm. "You just doubt my judgment. That's all."

Furious, she turned her back on her brother and waited until she'd heard the door close behind him before she turned a mortified look at Acton.

"I'm so sorry, Acton. I'm sorry for their behavior and sorry that I put you in this situation."

Letting out a long breath, he sat down on a wooden stool at the island. "You should've warned me about your brothers. If a person is expecting to be insulted, then it's not quite so bad when it does happen."

"They weren't insulting you. Not personally."

His short laugh told her exactly what he thought about that. "You could've fooled me. Do they always behave like jerks to your friends?"

Wishing she could melt into the floor and disappear, she walked over to him. "They didn't used to act like a trio of jackasses. But now…well, they're very protective of me. Because I… like they said, I've had some real stinking boyfriends in my life. And they're tired of seeing me end up on the losing end."

He frowned and his head moved slightly back and forth. "So they don't want you to date? Is that the problem?"

"Oh, they want me to date. They even want me to get married—eventually. But not before they make sure my man meets their expectations."

"Hell, that's like having three dads around trying to run your life. You're twenty-seven, Stephanie. You're old enough to choose your own man."

Her gaze dropped to the floor. "You're right. But so far I've been terrible at choosing. Or maybe I'm just not special enough to attract a good man."

His forefinger suddenly slipped beneath her chin and she sniffed as he lifted her face up to his.

"You're wrong, Stephanie. You're a special

woman. In so very many ways. You've just been unlucky in love, that's all."

She couldn't stop her eyes from misting over. Not to mention the fact that the touch of his finger on her chin was making her tremble all over. "You really think so?"

His smile was so tender that it made her heart hurt with longing.

"I know so. Because I've been unlucky in love, too. I understand what you've gone through."

Her lips parted with surprise. "You? That's not possible. I'm sure you have all kinds of women knocking on your door. And I can't imagine any one of them throwing you over for someone else."

He dropped his hand from her face, then speared his fingers through the dark blond curls falling near one eye. "Oh, Stephanie, sometimes I think you are far younger than me. Finding someone who fits you just right, who won't hurt you for any reason, who'll stand beside you through thick and thin—that's not an easy thing to do. I haven't managed to get it done…yet. Each time I think I'm getting close to finding that kind of woman, I've been disappointed. Big-time disappointed."

She placed her hand on his forearm, and as she did, their eyes met. The intimate clash caused her heart to skip a beat, and when she finally managed to speak, her voice sounded as if she'd just woken from a deep sleep.

"A few minutes ago, I'd wished that my brothers had never walked in here. And I'm still darned annoyed with all three of them. But now I'm almost glad. Otherwise, you might never have shared this with me. And it... I guess what I'm trying to say is that it makes me feel much closer to you. I hope you think that's a good thing."

A soft light glowed in his blue eyes. "I think it's good and great and every other stupendous adjective."

Laughing lightly, she leaned forward and kissed his cheek.

"What was that for?" he asked while rubbing his cheek with the tips of his fingers.

"It's my turn to thank you. Just for being Acton Donovan. And for not judging me by my brothers' behavior."

"You're very welcome, Stephanie. Now what do you say we start on the cupcakes? The sooner we get them baked, the sooner we can do a taste test."

"A taste test? Hmm. That's probably a good idea. If we bomb with our baking efforts, then I'll be forced to go to the bakery."

His grin oozed confidence. "With the two of us working together, we can't fail."

Chapter Six

Nearly an hour and a half later, after the cupcakes were cooled and frosted and the cookies packed away in a plastic storage container, Stephanie made coffee, then filled a basket with a thermos and a few of the sweets.

With Acton carrying Linus, and Stephanie toting the basket of goodies, she guided him to a wide foyer that connected a separate wing to the main section of the house. As they walked along, he noticed most of the hallway was made of plate glass. Beyond it, he could see footlights outlining a path through a perfectly landscaped courtyard.

When they reached a carved wooden door, she

opened it and gestured for him to enter. "This is my personal space," she told him. "I guess you'd call it my home within a home."

As she closed the door behind them, Acton gazed around the large, open area. The space was furnished as a sitting room, and though it was elaborate, it had a much homier feel than the monstrous kitchen they'd just left.

"Do you let the dogs in here?" Acton asked as he carried Linus to the middle of the room.

She walked over to him. "No. When I adopted Mack and Tallulah, they were both outdoor dogs. Mack is a terrier and a fierce digger. Tallulah is a dachshund and likes to show Mack she can dig even better than him. They'd be bored to tears if they were indoors. And, anyway, with two cats and the rabbit, it would be too crowded in here. Especially with Linus," she explained. "The dogs stay in a large fenced-in area at the back of the house. I'm having a longer run built for them so that they can go all the way to the stables and still be safely inside the fence. They love being around the horses, so that should make them really happy."

She gestured to an area where a round table was positioned near a floor-to-ceiling paned window. "I'll put our snacks here. Linus is sound asleep so let's put him in the bassinet."

While she deposited the basket on the table, Acton looked around for the bassinet. He spotted the portable hooded bed sitting a few feet away from a small fireplace, where apparently someone had lit a fire earlier in the evening. Now the logs had mostly turned to a pile of glowing red embers.

With Stephanie following close on his heels, Acton carried Linus over to the bassinet.

"If you'll give me the carrier," she suggested, "I'll hold it while you lift him out and put him to bed."

"I think I can do that." Careful to keep the baby's head supported, he scooped up Linus from the padded seat and gently laid him on a sheet printed with bright yellow ducks.

The baby seemed to sense he was finally in his own bed and as he squirmed slightly against the soft mattress, Acton smiled with satisfaction.

"Aww, look at him. He's looks comfortable now."

"He should be," Stephanie agreed. "His diaper is dry and his tummy is full. He'll sleep for hours."

She reached over and covered the baby with a pale blue blanket, and as she tucked the fabric around his tiny shoulders, Acton wondered how it would feel to have a baby son of his own. How would it feel to have a woman like Stephanie give him a child?

The thought had him rubbing a forefinger over Linus's dark hair. It was fine and soft and curled slightly on the ends. The vulnerability of the baby awed him in a way that surprised him. He'd never thought of himself as a daddy. Yet this little guy put a whole set of ideas in his head.

Acton had always admired his parents. Not just because they'd been happily married for so many years, but because they were so devoted to their children. They'd raised Acton and his three siblings with firm discipline and a wealth of love. And even though his father hadn't always been a perfect dad, Acton doubted he could ever fill his boots. As for his mother, Acton was pretty sure he could look to the ends of the earth and not find a woman with Faye Donovan's patient and nurturing soul.

"What are you thinking, Acton?"

Stephanie's soft question pulled Acton out of his thoughts and he glanced at her. The tender concern he saw on her features speared him right in the heart, and for a moment he was too struck by the feeling to even speak.

Finally, he said, "I, uh, was just thinking about my dad—wondering if I could ever be half the man that he is. He and Mom raised four of us. And just looking at little Linus makes me realize what an incredible task that must've been for them. I'm not sure I could do it, much less do it as well as they have."

"Parenting is a scary prospect. Especially if you want to do it right." She motioned toward the table, where their coffee, cupcakes and cookies were waiting. "Let's go sit. I'd like to hear about your family."

Once they were seated at the table, Stephanie poured two cups of coffee and passed out the desserts they'd baked.

Acton held up one of the cupcakes frosted with pink buttercream frosting. "It's a little lopsided, but who cares? I'm hoping the people who attend will have their mind on donations rather than the food."

Stephanie bit into a cookie. "Oh, this is scrumptious, Acton! No need to go by the bakery. I pronounce you a good cookie-maker."

"Thanks, but you helped, remember." He looked at her and winked. "I'll have to tell Grandma Hatti about this. She'll be proud. Because she's the one who taught me about cooking and baking. I might even manage to talk her into coming to the fundraiser. That is, if her arthritis isn't acting up."

She finished the last of the cookie and reached for a cupcake. "You said there were four of you. I've met Gina, so who are the other two?"

He nodded. "My brothers. They're both older than me. Shawn is after Gina and then Danny."

"Do your brothers work on your family ranch?" she asked.

"They do. Shawn is like me—he works on the ranch full-time. He mostly deals with the cattle while I tend to the cattle and the horses. Danny helps out on the ranch, too, but not on a daily basis. He has an outside job as a sales manager at the Travis County livestock auction."

"So your parents have always been together?"

Nodding, he said, "All these years and they're still crazy about each other. Their long, happy marriage is great, but it's also kind of daunting. It's a lot to live up to. Could be that's why me or my brothers have never tried it. None of us likes failing at anything." He glanced at her. "What about you, Stephanie? Are your parents still together?"

She reached for her coffee. "Yes. But my father, David, wasn't always married to my mother, Marci. He was first married to Penny. She's Callum and Dillon's mother. When Marci married Dad she already had two sons, Steven and Wiley. He adopted both of the boys and then he and Marci went on to have me and my triplet sisters. So you see, it's sort of a convoluted family. But all eight of us siblings get along fairly well."

"Hmm. So the brothers I met in the kitchen are actually two half-brothers and a stepbrother?"

"That's right. All of the brothers are half or step to us girls. But that doesn't stop them from being bossy," she added with a tight grimace. "I'm still upset with them for the way they treated you."

He shrugged. "Don't worry about it. I don't figure I'll be rubbing elbows with any of them, anyway. Besides, they could tell by looking at me that I'm not good enough to be your real boyfriend."

A look of disappointment flashed across her face and Acton wondered what might have caused the reaction. Maybe it was lingering regret over her brothers' behavior. In any case, he'd much rather see her smiling.

"One Minute" Survey

You get TWO books
<u>and</u> TWO Mystery Gifts...

Dear Reader,

Your opinions are important to us. So if you'll participate in our fast and free "One Minute" Survey, **YOU** can pick two wonderful books that **WE** pay for!

As a leading publisher of women's fiction, we'd love to hear from you. That's why we promise to reward you for completing our survey.

IMPORTANT: Please complete the survey and return it. We'll send your Free Books and Free Mystery Gifts right away. **And we pay for shipping and handling too!**

Thank you again for participating in our "One Minute" Survey. It really takes just a minute *We pay for EVERYTHING* (or less) to complete the survey... and your free books and gifts will be well worth it!

Sincerely,

Pam Powers

Pam Powers
for Reader Service

"One Minute" Survey

GET YOUR FREE BOOKS AND FREE GIFTS!

✓ Complete this Survey ✓ Return this survey

1 Do you try to find time to read every day?
☐ YES ☐ NO

2 Do you prefer stories with happy endings?
☐ YES ☐ NO

3 Do you enjoy having books delivered to your home?
☐ YES ☐ NO

4 Do you share your favorite books with friends?
☐ YES ☐ NO

YES! I have completed the above "One Minute" Survey. Please send me my Two Free Books and Two Free Mystery Gifts (worth over $20 retail). I understand that I am under no obligation to buy anything, as explained on the back of this card.

235/335 HDL GNN4

FIRST NAME	LAST NAME

ADDRESS

APT.#	CITY

STATE/PROV.	ZIP/POSTAL CODE

she hurried to the door, only to find Becky standing on the threshold.

"Becky, what are you doing?"

Her sister-in-law laughed. "What do you think? I'm babysitting Linus tonight, remember?"

She pushed the door wider so that Becky could enter. "Well, yes, I remember. And I'm still feeling very guilty that you're staying home with the kids while I'm out partying. On top of that, you and Callum are newlyweds and you should be celebrating Valentine's night together."

"You—partying? Ha! You're working a fund-raiser for the clinic. As for me and Callum, we're planning something special together for tomorrow night. Besides, I have two good reasons for spending the night at home. One, trying to corral the twins with a room full of dogs and cats would be disastrous. And two, Callum plans to use the gathering to talk business. That's not my idea of a romantic evening."

"Okay, I won't feel guilty anymore. But you didn't have to come for Linus. I was going to bring him and his things over to you."

Shaking her head, Becky followed Stephanie across the living room and down a short hallway to her bedroom. An array of glittery cocktail dresses was spread across the king-size bed, while in the middle of the dresses, Linus was lying on his belly, doing his best to paddle his arms and legs.

"You have enough to do with getting yourself ready," Becky told her. "By the way, the twins are excited to see Linus."

"Really? They can talk well enough to tell you that?"

"They're saying more words every day. I've taught them to say 'Linus.' Although it's coming out more like 'Nus' with the 'Li' missing."

Stephanie laughed. "How cute. Wouldn't it be wonderful if they could grow up as true cousins?"

Becky walked over to the bed. "It would. And who knows, that could possibly happen. Do you have his diaper bag packed?"

"I do. It's in the living room. Everything is in it, except for his bottles. They're still in the fridge."

"I'll get them," Becky told her, then made a slow perusal of the red dress Stephanie was wearing. The lacy sheath was body-hugging with long fitted sleeves and a boat neckline. "You look incredible in that red lace and those heels. I am so envious. You walk in those things like they're athletic shoes. I'd be teetering."

Laughing, Stephanie glanced down at the red high heels that fastened with a strap around her ankles. "I was going to ask you how I look. Is the dress appropriate? I don't want to be over-the-top, but I want to look like I'm going to a party instead of cleaning out kennels at the clinic."

"I'm giving you an A-plus. You look lovely. But

is that the way you're going to wear your hair—all frazzled out like that?"

Stephanie's hand automatically flew to her partially teased hair. "I was in the middle of doing my hair when you rang the doorbell. I'm going to wear it pinned up in curls on the crown. I had it that way last night and Acton liked it."

Becky smiled cleverly. "So you're trying to please Acton now? I don't think I'll tell Callum that just yet."

"I honestly don't care what you tell Callum," Stephanie said stiffly. "I'm still angry with all three of my brothers."

"Can't blame you for that. After you told me what they said to Acton, I'm honestly surprised he didn't try to bust all of them in the mouth."

Stephanie walked over to the dresser, where she'd laid out a comb and a stack of hairpins. "Acton is an easygoing guy. I'm grateful that he took it all in stride. Have I told you he's going to pick me up tonight and drive me to the fund-raiser?"

Becky walked up behind her and studied Stephanie's reflection in the mirror. "You didn't tell me. So is this supposed to be a date with you two? Has it come to that now?"

Stephanie shrugged. "We're not calling it a date. But it's the closest thing I've had to one in a long time."

"If that's the case, then you need to take extra

pains with your hair. I'm going to get Linus and get out of here so you can concentrate." She collected the baby from the bed, then on her way out, paused at the door. "Stephanie, I wouldn't worry. If Acton is the man I think he is, then all three of your brothers will be happy for you."

Turning away from the mirror, Stephanie looked gratefully at her sister-in-law. "Thanks, Becky. But like I told them, Acton and I are only friends—good friends."

Becky's smile was knowing. "I can't think of a better way to start a romance."

When Stephanie and Acton arrived at The Shoppes building, the parking area was already beginning to fill up with vehicles. Acton parked at the far end of the lot, then came around to help her out of the truck.

"Did you do gymnastics as a child?" he asked once she was standing on solid ground.

"No. Why?"

"Those heels. You'd have to be an acrobat to walk in them. But I'll say one thing, they're damned sexy." He flashed her a sizzling grin. "Everything about you tonight looks sexy."

No one had ever used that word to describe Stephanie. She'd been called pretty plenty of times, along with cute. But she'd never been called sexy. Hearing it from Acton's lips put a warm blush on her cheeks.

"Thank you, Acton. You look rather handsome yourself. I wasn't expecting you to get so dressed up."

He was wearing a dark, Western-cut suit with a white shirt. Black cowboy boots and a bolo tie with a silver-and-onyx slide completed the look that was masculine and classy at the same time.

He glanced down at himself. "I don't break out these clothes too often. But what the heck, it's Valentine's Day and we're going to a party. And speaking of Valentine's Day, I have a little something for you."

"For me?"

He opened the back door of the truck and pulled out a huge, beautiful bouquet of purple and yellow tulips arranged in an amber hobnail vase.

He said. "Considering the occasion, I should've probably gone with red and pink flowers. But I wanted you to have something different."

Stephanie was so touched by the unexpected gift that tears stung the back of her eyes.

He stepped closer and she accepted the bouquet from him. "What a lovely surprise, Acton! And the colors are gorgeous."

"My pleasure. I'm glad you like them."

Her gaze lifted from the tulips to scan his face and she noticed he'd left his hat in the truck. With his head bent slightly toward hers, the masculine scent of his hair swirled in her nostrils and acted on her senses like an aphrodisiac.

"I'd love to take the flowers in with me," she said,

while hoping her voice sounded steady. "But I'm afraid someone might confuse them as part of the decorations and they'd end up in the wrong hands."

"I'd hate for that to happen. Let's just leave them here. Since the night is cool they should be fine."

By the time he returned the bouquet back to the truck and locked the vehicle, Stephanie's knees were quivering and she latched a hand on his forearm to steady herself.

"Thank you, Acton, for the lovely flowers. Do you mind if I hang on to you while we walk to the building? I'm not used to these heels."

His eyes twinkling, he pressed a hand over hers. "I'm all yours."

All hers? For this one special night, Stephanie was going to let herself believe him.

Chapter Seven

The old Woolworth's five-and-dime building had been a part of downtown Rambling Rose for many years. Now it was little more than town history. In the past months, Fortune Brothers Construction had purchased and transformed the old structure into a group of elaborate units named The Shoppes at Rambling Rose. And with none of the businesses opened yet, Stephanie's brothers had offered the spacious lobby for the Paws and Claws fund-raiser.

Stephanie regarded their offer as a charitable act, but Acton was more inclined to believe their generosity had been a two-fold arrangement. Not only would the donation put them in a favorable light with the townspeople, but it also gave them a perfect opportunity to show off the impressive makeover of the building.

To be fair, that one awkward meeting in the Fame and Fortune kitchen was hardly enough for Acton to actually size up Stephanie's brothers. So he hardly had the right to belittle their motives. For Stephanie's sake, he hoped their intentions were heartfelt.

Now, as the two of them stepped inside the glass-enclosed lobby of The Shoppes, they both gazed in amazement at the elegant space. Beyond the Italian tiled floor and the artistic waterfall in the center of the space, yards of tulle in pink, red and white were draped from the ceiling, along with clusters of paper hearts. The dogs that were up for adoption were all wearing red sweaters, while the cat cages were festooned with paper hearts and balloons with enough helium to keep them floating out of the reach of their playful claws.

Love songs were playing over the impressive sound system, while along one wall, a dessert buffet had been set up, including the cookies and cupcakes that Stephanie and Acton had baked the night before.

"Wow! This looks nothing like the old building that I remember!" Acton exclaimed. "The room, the decorations—this is impressive!"

"It does look nice," Stephanie agreed. "But I'm more enthused about this huge crowd. And I see that Callum and Steven have already arrived."

Acton followed the direction of her gaze until he spotted the two men standing several feet away. Callum appeared to be in deep conversation with a man that served on the Rambling Rose city council. Steven turned his head just enough for him to catch sight of Stephanie and Acton. Even at a distance Acton could see the man's eyes narrow skeptically.

"I don't think Steven is too happy about seeing us together like this," Acton told her, while privately he was fighting the urge to walk over and tell the eldest Fortune brother to go to hell.

Unconcerned, she replied, "That's too bad. We're here together. Aren't we?"

Thankfully, the sweetness that radiated from Stephanie had a soothing effect on Acton and he told himself it didn't matter what her brothers thought of him. All that mattered was what she thought of him, and tonight she was looking at him with a warm, inviting glow in her eyes.

"We're definitely here together," he said. "Let's go mingle and see if we can talk some of these people into adopting a few pets."

The two had barely managed to move a few feet into the milling crowd when Dayna intercepted them.

"Is this turnout incredible or what?" she asked as she nibbled from the small plate she was carrying. "I honestly think most of the guests are here to see what Stephanie's brothers have done to this place.

If it wasn't full of dog and cat cages, it would look like a room taken right out of a palace."

"As long as people are donating money to Paws and Claws, that's the important thing," Stephanie said.

"Don't worry, Steph. The night is just getting started and I've already seen lots of money being dropped into the pot," Dayna assured her.

"That's good news," Stephanie replied, then flashed a glance in the direction of Callum and Steven. "You can bet I'm expecting my brothers to contribute to the cause. And if I don't see amounts involving at least four digits written on their checks, I'm going to disown them."

Acton whistled under his breath. "Sounds like you have high expectations."

"I do from my brothers. They can afford it."

"My brother donated a check with four numbers," Dayna said with a laugh. "But there was a decimal in the middle."

"Every donation is appreciated and welcome," Stephanie told her coworker. "No matter the amount."

Dayna turned a sage smile on Acton. "It's easy to forget that she's a Fortune," she said, then suddenly waved at someone across the room. "Excuse me, you two. My mom is signaling me. I'll catch up with you later."

Frowning thoughtfully, Stephanie watched Dayna

disappear into the crowd. "Sometimes she can say the weirdest things."

Acton said, "I understood what she was getting at. I feel the same way. You don't come across as anything like your high-rolling brothers."

She let out a short laugh. "Thank you. I think."

Acton's gaze made another trip around the room, which had been lavishly refurbished with plenty of plate glass and strategically placed lighting. From what Stephanie had told him, there were already several upscale retail businesses ready to move in. The change might be grand for some of the citizens of Rambling Rose, but Acton couldn't see it drawing in the regular, hardworking folks who'd originally founded the town.

"Judging by this building, I agree that your brothers could write a sizable check to Paws and Claws." He cast her a wry look. "I just hope you're not expecting four numbers without the decimal from me."

Her eyes widened with dismay. "Oh, no, Acton. You've already given more than enough. First your help baking and then your help hauling some of the animals over here. That means as much or more than money."

Shrugging, he wondered why it was so important to him to impress her. He sure as hell couldn't do it with money. But maybe, just maybe, she was different enough from her brothers not to care what was in his bank account.

"I didn't do that much. But I have been wondering about something. Where is Buddy? Isn't he going to be given the chance to be adopted? Or did Dr. Neil want to wait until his cast was removed?"

A smug smile came over her pretty face. "Dr. Neil took Buddy's cast off yesterday. But the dog didn't need to come to the party tonight to find himself a home. Someone has already made arrangements to adopt him."

"That's great news. After all Buddy has been through, I hope it's someone who appreciates him."

"It is." She smiled. "I confess, that someone is me," she told him. "Buddy is going to be my dog."

Acton wasn't surprised in the least. Stephanie was the nurturing sort and her heart was too big for her own good. It was no wonder that men had taken advantage of her in the past, he thought. And the idea that she'd been hurt in such a way sickened Acton to the core of his being. Obviously it had sickened her brothers, too. But that didn't give them the right to assume Acton was just another jerk out to get whatever he could from their sister.

"I should have known," Acton said to her. "So Buddy is going to have to learn how to dig holes like Mack and Tallulah."

She laughed and he noticed how the pearl drops she was wearing in her ears swung against her smooth neck. He'd never seen a real live seductress before, but he figured Stephanie looked very close to being one tonight. From the moment he'd picked her up at the Fame and Fortune Ranch, he'd been staring at her like a besotted buffoon.

"I'm sure they'll teach Buddy all about the art of digging," she said, then looped her arm through his. "Let's go see what we can find on the buffet table. I'm starving."

The party was still going on two hours later, although a large portion of guests had already departed with animals in tow. To Stephanie's delight, all of the animals, except for one young female cat, had found forever homes.

Grizabella was still sitting in a wire cage, watching people pass her by and, no doubt, wondering why she was the only animal left behind.

The gray-and-white feline was beautiful and sweet, but no one had seemed to want her because she was blind in one eye. The handicap didn't bother Grizabella in the least. She could run and play just as well as any of the two-eyed cats. It was the humans who wanted to put limitations on her.

Stephanie spoke softly to the cat, while stroking her little nose through the wire slats. "I promise you, Grizabella, I'll find you a good home. One where you'll be appreciated for the fine girl you are."

Stephanie hardly needed to take on another cat, especially since she'd signed on for Buddy. But she couldn't bear the thought of Grizabella being left behind.

"Has no one taken Grizabella yet?"

Stephanie looked around to see Acton had walked up behind her. He offered her one of the foam cups he was carrying.

"Thanks. I needed this." She took a careful sip of the hot coffee, then answered his question. "Unfortunately no. And it makes me want to cry, Acton. Just look how beautiful she is."

"She's as pretty as a June mornin'," he agreed.

Leaning toward the cage, he stuck a finger through the wire and wiggled it to attract Grizabella's attention. Instead of pawing at his finger, Grizabella decided she'd rather give it a loving swipe with her tongue.

Acton laughed. "Hey, I think she likes me."

"Of course, she likes you. She's a sweetheart."

He continued to waggle his finger and Grizabella rubbed her cheek against it.

"You know, I've always wanted a cat," he said after a moment. "I think the two of us would be great pals."

Stephanie was shocked. She'd recognized from the first day he'd brought Seymour to the clinic that, where animals were concerned, he had a big heart. But that didn't necessarily mean he was generous enough to take on an extra pet just because it needed a home.

"Really? You'd give a one-eyed cat a home?"

"I don't see Grizabella as a one-eyed cat. I see her as a pretty and loving kitty. My only concern is Seymour and that jealous streak of his."

He didn't see Grizabella as handicapped. Maybe it was silly of her, but suddenly she was seeing that sign around his neck that read Good.

"Oh, I think Seymour won't have a problem with Grizabella. In fact, I have a feeling that he'll like the company." She gave him an encouraging smile. "I'd be glad to come over and help you get the two of them acquainted."

"You'd do that?"

"Certainly." She glanced questioningly at the cat. "So? Is she going to be yours?"

"Sure. I couldn't tell either of you no. So Grizabella is going to the Diamond D to live with me."

Too happy to contain herself, Stephanie rose on the tips of her toes and kissed his cheek. "You're a wonderful man, Acton."

Grinning, he was about to reply, when voices suddenly rose from somewhere behind them. Both Stephanie and Acton turned to see Steven and Callum in what appeared to be a heated discussion with a tall woman dressed in a Navy blue, glen-plaid business suit. A curtain of straight dark hair hung against her back.

"Isn't that the mayor my brothers are talking to?" Stephanie asked.

Acton squinted at the trio. "Right. Ellie Hernandez. And from the sound of things, your brothers are disagreeing with her about something."

Slipping her hand into Acton's, Stephanie lowered her voice so that only he could hear. "Let's move over a few steps and maybe we can hear exactly what they're discussing."

Using the same hushed tone, he playfully scolded, "Stephanie, you want to eavesdrop!"

"So what? We're in a public place and those three aren't exactly trying to be discreet, are they?"

Acton glanced at the trio as Stephanie pulled him in front of a stack of empty animal crates. "Well, no," he answered. "Looks like they've forgotten they're at a public function."

Across the way, the young attractive mayor was waving her hand in a circular motion. "Yes, I agree," she said. "The renovations you've completed on this property are amazing. Everyone can see that. My problem is this—The Shoppes look more appropriate for Rodeo Drive in Hollywood than our little town of Rambling Rose!"

Scowling, Steven said, "As the mayor, you should be proud that your town can boast of such improvements. Don't you believe the people of Rambling Rose deserve to have nice businesses and buildings?"

The woman snorted. "I happen to believe if an election was held tomorrow, most of the citizens would vote to run Fortune Brothers Construction out of town on a rail!"

Callum chuckled. "Steven, I think Mayor Hernandez has been watching too many old Westerns. Maybe we should be worried about getting tarred and feathered, too, before they put us on the rail," he joked.

Stephanie cringed. "He's hardly winning any points with her," she whispered to Acton.

"From what I know about the lady, she's no pushover," Acton whispered back.

As if on cue, the mayor retorted, "I hardly think this is anything to joke about, Mr. Fortune. It's also obvious to me that neither of you understands what it means to be Texan. We don't take kindly to outsiders moving in and trying to change our towns, or our lifestyles."

Steven said, "I can't believe that any true Texan would be opposed to progress. And that's what my brothers and I are trying to do here. Make improvements to Rambling Rose."

"You're not being honest, Mr. Fortune. You're trying to make money. That's what you and your brothers are all about. And I don't like the idea of your profit coming at the expense of my citizens."

"Really, Mayor Hernandez, we're not vultures. We want what's good for the people of Rambling Rose just as much as you do," Callum said, attempting to assure her. "And the last I heard, capitalism isn't a crime. That's how this great country of ours was built."

"I've studied history, Mr. Fortune," the mayor said in an icy voice. "Especially Texas history. The battle of the Alamo exemplifies how Texans fought and died for what they wanted. Maybe the both of you should take a lesson from that. Now if you'll excuse me, I have other people to see."

The mayor walked away and so did Stephanie's brothers. Once all three were out of sight, Acton whistled under his breath. "Man, oh, man, steam was coming out of her ears."

"She was seething, all right," Stephanie agreed. "This reminds me how glad I am that I'm not a part of Fortune Brothers Construction. I don't think I could sleep at night. I can already imagine what kind of obstacles the mayor is going to throw up when they start making plans for the hotel and all the other things they want to build around town."

"Well, Callum might joke about the mayor watching too many Westerns, but they need to realize if they get her riled up enough she might just turn into another Annie Oakley."

Regret turned down the corners of Stephanie's lips. "I wish my brothers could be…a little more Texan. Like you, Acton. Then I think they'd understand what people around here really want for their town."

"Hey, you two, I think Dr. Neil wants to start wrapping up this shindig."

They both looked around to see Carla popping a chocolate Hershey's Kiss into her mouth. The receptionist looked exceptionally pretty tonight, Stephanie thought. Her dress was blue velvet and her brown hair, which she normally wore in a bun, rested in soft curls upon her shoulders.

Carla was far more suitable for Acton, Stephanie thought. She came from a ranching family. The two of them had much more in common. And yet, Acton didn't seem to pay any more attention to Carla than he did the other women on the Paws and Claws staff—a fact that still amazed her. Why had he singled out Stephanie? Because he honestly thought she was special? Or because her last name was Fortune?

When are you going to get that out of your mind, Stephanie? Not everybody gives a damn about your last name. Not everyone cares about your money. And if that's what you think about Acton, you need to walk away from him right now.

Ignoring the mocking voice in her head, Stephanie said to Carla, "I think everyone has donated that's planning to. So it probably is time to get everything loaded and back to the clinic."

"I see Grizabella is the only animal left," Carla said, glancing in the direction of the cat cage. "Too bad no one wanted her."

Stephanie smiled proudly at Acton. "But someone did want her," she told Carla. "Acton is adopting her."

Surprised, Carla looked at him. "Really? I'm glad you felt sorry for her."

Acton frowned. "But I don't feel sorry for Grizabella. I don't believe she needs my sympathy. She needs my love."

Clearly embarrassed, Carla said, "Excuse me. I never thought of it that way. You're a nice guy, Acton."

She turned and walked away and Acton let out a long sigh. "Sometimes I can be a real jerk. I should've never said that to her. At least, not in that way. She meant well. It's just that it annoys the hell out of me when people dwell on the wrong instead of the right."

"I wouldn't worry about Carla. She'll think about what you said and in the long run it will help her. Now me, I'm the one who'd like to slither out of here without being seen. I can only hope the rest of the room didn't hear the things being said between my brothers and the mayor. But I have the feeling most of the guests did hear their conversation. My family is going to be the gossip around town," she said, then let out a caustic laugh. "What am I thinking? They already are the town gossip."

Draping his arm around her shoulders, he urged her over to Grizabella's cage. "Come on, forget all that. Let's tell Grizabella she's finished with that nerve-wracking cat room at the clinic. From now on, she's going to be a ranch cat."

Stephanie laughed and thought how she'd never met any man that made her feel so good—until Acton had walked into her life.

The hands on Acton's watch were nearing midnight when he finally pulled the truck to a stop in front of the massive Fortune estate.

After helping Stephanie out of the truck, he walked her to her private wing and stood to one side, holding the bouquet of tulips, while she unlocked the door.

"Would you like to come in for a few minutes?" she asked. "I can make coffee…or something."

Acton was sorely tempted to accept her offer, but tonight he couldn't trust himself. Tonight, something had happened to him and he couldn't yet figure out what it was or why it was making him feel so differently. He only knew that being alone with Stephanie might change everything between them and he wasn't sure if he, or she, was ready for that.

"Thanks, Stephanie, but I think I'd better get on home." He handed her the vase of flowers. "I don't want to leave Grizabella in the truck too long. She'll think she's being deserted."

"Oh, that's right. You have Grizabella. She was so quiet on the ride over here that I almost forgot about her."

She smiled tentatively at him and Acton inwardly groaned as his gaze focused on her moist lips.

"I, uh, had a great time tonight," he said. "And Paws and Claws raised more money than any of us expected. That's a good thing."

"I had a great time, too." She touched one of the purple tulips. "And I was given a lovely Valentine. Thank you for the bouquet, Acton. And thank you for wanting to love Grizabella. I'm learning you're a real softy."

He gave her a lopsided grin. "There's a lot you haven't learned about me...yet, that is."

She drew in a deep breath and Acton got the impression that she was nervous about something. Him? He hoped not. He wanted her to feel very much at home with him. He wanted her to feel like being with him was as right as him taking Grizabella.

"Really?" she asked. "Like what?"

"Like how much I've wanted to do this—for a very long time."

"This?"

His hands curved over her shoulders and the warmth radiating from her body urged him to draw her closer. "Taking you in my arms and kissing you."

She sucked in a breath, but he didn't wait to see if she was going to make any sort of reply. Instead, he pulled her into the circle of his arms and lowered his lips to hers.

Acton had meant to keep the kiss short and sweet.

He'd simply wanted a brief taste of her, just to let her know where his thoughts were headed.

But it didn't work out exactly that way. As soon as their lips made contact, some sort of explosion detonated inside him. And inside Stephanie, too, apparently. Before he recognized what was happening, their mouths were fused together and his hands were tugging her forward until the tulips were very nearly crushed between their bodies.

Kissing Stephanie was like dipping his tongue into a pot of wild honey. The smooth sweetness clung to his lips, making him want more and more.

It wasn't until he heard a tiny moan in her throat that reality returned. And even then it took a mountain of strength to tear his mouth from hers and set her back from him.

"I, uh, think I'd better be going, Stephanie."

"Going?"

She sounded just as dazed as Acton felt, and for a split second he wondered if he'd gone crazy. He wasn't built to ignore the passion in a woman's kiss. Everything inside his body was screaming at him to kiss her again, to take her into her fancy house and make hot, wild love to her.

But Stephanie wasn't just any woman. And he wasn't the same man who'd taken a woman to bed just because it felt good. No, somewhere in the past week, she'd changed him, and now all he wanted was to cherish and protect her.

Oh, damn.

Those were the things a husband wanted to do for his wife—for the woman he loved! The idea that Acton was falling that hard for Stephanie, rattled his senses.

"Yes. Going," he repeated huskily. "Tonight—at this moment—I think that's best for both of us." Bending his head, he brushed a kiss to the corner of her lips, then another one on her cheek.

Her hand latched on to his arm as though she didn't want to let him go. But then her eyes slowly opened and a tempting little smile curved her lips.

"Yes. Best for both of us. That's what I want, too," she whispered. "Good night, Acton."

She turned and entered the house and Acton stood there staring at the closed door, and wondered how long it was going to take his senses to come back to earth.

Chapter Eight

"Mom, do you have any sardines or tuna?"

Standing at the kitchen sink, Faye Donovan, a tall woman with short blond hair and a gentle face, turned away from the pot she was scrubbing to cast a concerned look at Acton.

"Son, are things getting so tight that you've run out of groceries and resorted to eating peanut butter and crackers?"

Acton laughed. "No, Mom. I have enough to buy myself a cabinet full of groceries. I just haven't taken the time to go to the supermarket. Dad has kept me and Shawn pretty tied up with that new cross fence we've been building."

"Yes, once your father makes up his mind to do something, he wants it done yesterday. But maybe that's a good thing. I never could stand procrastination. Especially in a man."

Was that what Acton was doing? He wondered. Three days had passed since the night of the Paws and Claws Valentine's party and he'd not seen or messaged Stephanie even once.

Oh, he'd wanted to. Everything inside him was aching to see her again. To kiss her and allow the passion he'd felt budding between them the other night to burst into full bloom. But he'd turned into a coward. What if he did make love to Stephanie? Where was that going to lead them? As far as he could see, it was going to lead to heartache. And then he'd end up being one more name on that list of no-accounts who'd already broken her heart.

Acton chugged down the last of the ice water he'd poured for himself. "The sardines and tuna aren't for me, Mom. I guess I forgot to tell you. I have a cat now. I adopted her the other night at the Valentine shindig."

Faye turned back to the saucepan soaking in the sink of sudsy water. "Oh, yes, I meant to tell you that I sent a donation to them through the mail. After wrestling around with that two-year-old colt all afternoon, your father was just too tired to get dressed up to go. To tell you the truth, I was a little disappointed. It was Valentine's Day and we haven't gone anywhere dressed up in a long time."

"Aww, Mom, that's awful." He walked over and wrapped an affectionate arm around her shoulders. "You should've let me know. You could've gone with me."

"It wouldn't have been the same. And, anyway, your father made it up to me. Look at this."

After wiping her hands on a dish towel, she lifted the right one and flashed a ruby-and-diamond ring at him.

"Isn't that something?"

Acton whistled. "I'll say. That must have cost Dad a couple of calves!"

"Oh, you!" She poked a finger in Acton's midsection. "A woman doesn't want a man who's always practical. She needs romance once in a while."

Would a ring from him put a smile on Stephanie's face? Not an engagement ring, but one that meant she was more than a friend? No. A ring would just complicate things, he thought. Besides, she'd probably laugh at any gemstone he could afford.

"I'll keep that in mind, Mom. Now what about the sardines or tuna? I'm desperate. Grizabella is hiding under the bed and the only way I can tempt her out is with fish. I've used every can I have."

Faye walked over and opened the door to a floor-to-ceiling pantry. "Was she a feral cat or something?"

"No. At Paws and Claws she didn't seem timid at

all. But when I got her home and she took one look at Seymour walking through the house, she was traumatized. Now I can't convince her that he's harmless."

She carried three cans of tuna over to where he stood next to the cabinet. "Well, I'm not so sure this is going to convince her. But you're welcome to it. Maybe she just needs a female voice to coax her out. I'd come down and help, but Gina wants me to do some mending for her tonight."

A female voice. Yes, Acton knew exactly what female voice Grizabella needed to hear to calm her fears. But that meant inviting Stephanie over to his house. He wasn't sure he was ready for that.

Coward. Since when has a woman caused you to develop a yellow streak down your back? You're acting like an idiot!

"Thanks, Mom, but I'll manage somehow."

As he started out of the room, Faye called to him.

"Acton, speaking of the Valentine's party, I heard you were seen with a pretty young lady with the last name of Fortune."

"Who told you that?"

"Joyce Crandall. You know, the woman who plays piano at church."

"I've never said more than two words to her in my life. What is she? A busybody or something?"

"No. She just thought I might want to know that you're associating with the Fortunes. It's not like

everyone in the county hasn't been talking about
the rich family that's moved in and started taking
over the town. Frankly, your father and I are a little
surprised you haven't said anything to us about this
young woman."

Acton should've known this was coming. Living
in a small town, people talked—even when there was
nothing to talk about. In this case, Joyce and every
other guest at the Valentine party had probably noticed the way Acton had been glued to Stephanie's
side the entire evening.

"Why should I have said anything? Stephanie is
just a friend. A good friend. There's nothing more
to tell."

Faye was unconvinced, which hardly surprised
Acton. When it came to her sons, she'd always been
able to read between the lines.

"So you two are just friends. Looks like I've been
concerned about nothing."

Acton walked back to the center of the kitchen.
"Concerned? Why would you be concerned that I'm
friends with a member of the Fortune family?"

She grimaced, then made a helpless gesture with
her hands. "I didn't mean it exactly like that. But
there's been so much talk about the family and I remember reading about the trouble up in Austin with
that bunch of Fortunes who have the tech business.
His ex-wife was trying to kill him. She burned down
part of their house and injured her own son."

Stephanie hadn't mentioned anything like this to Acton and he wasn't one to keep up with that sort of news. He did well to tune in to the market report when he drank his first cup of coffee in the morning. And the only reason he bothered with the market news was to keep account of cattle and hay prices.

He told his mother, "That has nothing to do with this family of Fortunes."

"Probably not," Faye agreed. "But I guess my concern is…well, none of you kids ever associated with a family who had that kind of drama connected to it. Or was worth the kind of money they're worth. They're just not your style, Acton. And I don't mean that in an insulting way. I mean it as a compliment. You're too good for them."

Acton groaned. "Oh, Mom, you're biased. And for your information, Stephanie isn't what you think. She's kind and sweet and very down-to-earth. She works as a vet assistant, for Pete's sake." He kissed her cheek and started out of the room. "I've got to go. Grizabella is under the bed." Pausing at the doorway, he added, "And don't worry about me. I'm not being sucked in by a diabolical family."

Groaning, she waved him toward the door. "Get out of here. Go charm your cat."

"Stephanie, are you feeling sick?"

The sound of Dr. Neil's voice interrupted her thoughts and she glanced around to see the veterinarian had finished removing a large cyst from a cat and was in the process of taking off his gloves. At some point during the surgical procedure Stephanie's mind must have wandered.

She blinked her eyes and mentally shook herself. "I'm fine, Dr. Neil. Did I do something wrong?"

The kind vet gave her a reassuring smile. "I don't remember you ever doing anything wrong, Stephanie. And you've never gotten sick at the sight of blood. But you look a little pale and strained. I hope you're not coming down with a virus. There are several strains running rampant around town right now."

She was coming down with something all right, and it was scaring the living daylights of her. Plain and simple, she was lovesick and she had no clue how to cure herself of the malady.

"I'm just a bit tired, that's all. Don't worry, Dr. Neil."

He gave her shoulder a kindly pat. "We've had a hell of day today," he said, then lowered his voice to a whisper. "And don't tell anyone, but you've worked circles around the other assistants."

The doctor's compliment put a smile on her face. No one, especially her brothers, understood how important her job was to her. Helping to make an animal healthy and happy was gratifying and rewarding to her. Just like being Linus's mother filled her with overwhelming love and protectiveness.

"Thank you, Dr. Neil. I'll keep that a secret." She

gestured to the black cat on the operating table. At the moment, he was still under anesthesia, but would soon be waking.

"Are you all finished with Chester?"

"All finished. Give him a shot of seven-day antibiotic and put him in recovery. As soon as he wakes up, he can go home. Ruby is probably going to burst into tears when she sees the hide cut off his back, but just reassure her that after a few days it will close up nicely. Oh, and send a bottle of antiseptic home with her to help keep down the bacteria. But no charge. The poor woman can't afford it. And just so you know, I haven't made any typos on her bill. I'm making adjustments on the cost of Chester's treatment."

Ruby, Chester's owner, was a willow-thin woman in her early seventies with graying auburn hair and thick tortoiseshell-frame glasses. From the woman's prior visits, Stephanie had learned Ruby was a widow. After her husband's death, she'd been forced to sell her home and move into a cheap rental house on the edge of town. However, that hadn't stopped Ruby from going around picking up stray cats and giving them a home, even when she struggled to feed herself.

"Yes, Dr. Neil. I'll take care of it."

After Stephanie transferred the cat to the recovery room, she collected a bottle of antiseptic from the supplies cabinet and made her way to the waiting area.

Before she walked over to give Ruby the news about Chester, she stopped by the checkout desk, where Sheri was studying a spreadsheet on the computer screen.

Stifling a yawn, she turned her attention to Stephanie. "Oh, what a day. You have a bill for Chester?"

"I do." She handed Sheri the sheet of paper with the itemized charges. "And I want you to put the charge to my account. I'll pay for it before I leave work this evening."

"Stephanie, don't be such a softy!" Sheri scolded. "You can't take care of every hard-luck person who walks in here!"

Stephanie glanced over her shoulder to where Ruby was reading one of the magazines left scattered around the waiting area.

"Dr. Neil is barely charging her anything. So I'll pick up the rest. She deserves help. And don't let on to Ruby about any of this. Just tell her that Dr. Neil didn't have to do that much to Chester." Sheri opened her mouth to object again, but Stephanie cut her off. "Just play along."

Sheri shrugged. "Okay, whatever you say," she said, then went on before Stephanie had a chance to walk away. "I've been meaning to tell you how gorgeous you looked the other night at the Valentine's party. Seeing you in your work clothes around here, I would've never imagined you in lace and high heels. You surprised me."

Even though Stephanie had grown up in a wealthy family and had often had to look the part at her parents' dinner parties, she'd never been the glamour-girl type. And since she'd moved to Rambling Rose, she'd purposely kept her image low-key. She didn't want to give the locals any reason to say she was trying to show off.

"Sometimes I surprise myself, Sheri."

"Well, having a guy like Acton Donovan at your side is like having a gorgeous accessory. You two looked mighty friendly, too."

Stephanie didn't have time for frivolous gossip. Especially when she figured Acton would soon be moving his fickle attention to some other woman around town. Maybe he already had, she thought dismally. Ever since he'd plastered that scorching kiss on her lips, she'd not seen or heard a word from him.

"We are mighty friendly," Stephanie replied stiffly. "But that's all."

Sheri laughed. "Steph, don't try to kid a kidder, or trick a trickster, or however that old saying goes. You've been going around all day with stars in your eyes. And who could blame you? If Acton looked at me the way he looks at you, I'd have to wear sunglasses even in the dark."

Stars in her eyes? Dr. Neil had already asked her if she was getting sick. Her emotions must really be getting out of hand.

"I think you need glasses, period," Stephanie told her, then quickly headed over to Ruby.

She had just given the woman an update about Chester's condition when she felt her cell phone vibrate in the pocket of her mustard-colored cardigan.

I need help with Grizabella. Can you come this evening?

After three days without a word from the man, he was asking for her help? Stephanie knew she should be annoyed with him. She should tell him to get one of his many girlfriends to help him with Grizabella. But she couldn't do that. Not when his message had her heart singing like a happy bird. It was ridiculous.

Without hesitation, she typed in a reply and punched the send arrow. I'll be over after work.

"You're smiling," Ruby said. "Must be good news."

Stephanie looked at the older woman, who was still sitting on the short couch. "I suppose it is good," she said, then added thoughtfully, "Would you mind if I asked you something personal, Ruby?"

"Honey, you can ask me anything."

"How long were you married?"

A fond smile creased her face. "Forty years. And that wasn't near enough time with my Stanley. When you're married to someone who's also your friend, time is precious. You're too young to appreciate that advice now, but later on you'll understand."

"So your advice is to marry someone you like," Stephanie said. "How did you know Stanley was the one?"

"His eyes. He looked at me with kindness. There has to be more than flames and sparks to make things last between a man and a woman."

Stephanie hadn't thought about it in exactly those terms, but she understood the advice Ruby was trying to convey. There had to be more than hot chemistry to make a relationship long-lasting. And perhaps that's where she'd gone wrong in the past. She'd let the thrill of a man's kiss cloud her judgment. Which meant, if Acton did kiss her again, she could enjoy it, but it would be a mistake to allow the passion to take control of her senses.

"I'll think about that, Ruby. Thank you for sharing it with me." She gave the woman an appreciative smile. "Now, I'll go see if Chester is awake. I'm sure he's going to be more than ready for you to take him home."

The Donovan Ranch was located north of Rambling Rose, an area of the countryside Stephanie hadn't yet seen since she'd moved to Texas. Now as she drove along a wide, graveled road, she was impressed with the beauty of sloping green pastures dotted with enormous live oaks and wide ponds full from the winter rains. Herds of black cows, many with calves at their sides, grazed on the grass that was managing to survive the cooler winter weather.

During one of their conversations, Acton had expressed to Stephanie just how much he loved the ranch and would never dream of living anywhere else. Now as she drove slowly through the property, she understood why he felt so devoted to the place. It was a pastoral paradise.

When Stephanie finally spotted the old farmhouse where Acton lived, twilight was spreading across the wide lawn and the two-story clapboard structure. She parked near the gate of a fence made of woven wire and cedar post, and was in the process of collecting Linus from the backseat of the car, when she heard a loud bark directly behind her.

Glancing over her shoulder, she saw Seymour racing toward her.

"Seymour! Hey, boy!"

As soon as the dog recognized her voice, he skidded to a halt and his bushy tail began to whirl in a happy circle.

Stephanie kneeled down and urged the dog to join her. "Come here, Seymour. Come here and let me look at you."

The dog trotted over to her and Stephanie smiled as she rubbed his furry head. If it hadn't been for Seymour, she doubted she and Acton would have ever met. The idea seemed unimaginable now.

After giving Seymour a final pat between the ears, she lifted Linus from his car seat. She made sure the baby was carefully covered from the cold, then gathered his diaper bag with her free hand and used her hip to shut the car door.

"Okay, Seymour. I'm ready. Let's go."

With a whine of approval, the dog took off in a proud trot toward the house. By the time Stephanie reached the front entrance, Seymour was already waiting at the door, his tail thumping excitedly against the board planks that made up the porch floor.

After knocking on the screen door, she glanced down at the dog. "Seymour, I don't see any bald spots on your pretty fur, so your scratching days must be over."

Seymour responded with a bark and she was laughing in response when Acton opened the door. The warm smile on his face welcomed her.

"Hi, Stephanie. Please, come in." He stepped past the door to join her on the porch and Seymour took the opportunity to dash through Acton's legs and straight into the house.

"Hello, Acton. Sorry I'm running so late. We had a very busy day at the clinic."

After the way they'd parted the other night, she'd thought it would be awkward to face him this evening. But as soon as he stepped close and their eyes met, everything felt familiar and right.

He looked at me with kindness.

Ruby's words echoed in her mind and she realized Acton often looked at her with kindness and so much more. Did that mean he was the one?

"No problem," he said. "I'm just glad you could make it. Let me carry Linus for you."

He reached for the baby and Stephanie handed him over. Immediately he peeked under the edge of the blanket at Linus's face.

"I'm glad you brought Linus with you. I've missed seeing the little guy. Just about as much as I've missed seeing you." He turned his smile away from the baby and directed it at her. "I forgot to give you directions. How did you find the place?"

"Dayna told me. She knows where everybody lives."

She followed him into the house and he closed the door behind them. Stephanie's gaze was immediately glued to his tall, lean body dressed in jeans and a black T-shirt that clung to his hard-as-steel abs.

Ever since he'd kissed her the night of the fundraiser, she'd not been able to forget how it had felt to be crushed against all that sinewy muscle. Nor had she forgotten the incredibly alluring taste of his mouth searching hers.

"Uh, you said you've missed me. If that's true, why haven't I heard from you before now?"

A sheepish look crossed his face. "I thought I should give you a breather."

She lifted her chin to a challenging angle. "Really? I thought you'd decided that I was such a terrible kisser you didn't want to waste your time with me anymore."

His jaw dropped. "Are you serious?"

"Yes, I guess I am," she admitted, while wondering where she'd found the nerve to bring up the subject. Most likely, Acton wasn't used to a woman questioning his actions, but Stephanie had decided it was time to learn just where things stood with them. "I mean, you took off the other night like a pack of wild dogs was on your heels. And then when I didn't hear from you, what was I supposed to think?"

Groaning ruefully, he stepped toward her. "It wasn't like what you're thinking, Steph. I was... I knew I had to get out of there or we, uh, or something might've happened that neither one of us was ready for."

Ready? For a long time now, she'd been ready for him to reach for her, to make love to her. But obviously he wasn't feeling that same urgent need. That should be enough to put a damper on her feelings, to show her that he wasn't looking for anything serious. Yet it wasn't enough to stop the longing that had been building inside her. Just looking at him made her think about things she'd never experienced before. He made her long for the things that she'd always wanted in her life. Yes, maybe her mind could recognize she was going too fast, too soon. But that wasn't what her heart was telling her.

She sighed. "I understand. It's just that a girl takes these things—like kissing—to heart, Acton."

A gentle smile suddenly crinkled the corners of his eyes. "You need to stop worrying. You're a fantastic kisser, Stephanie."

If any other man had said such a thing to her, she would've been horribly embarrassed, but with Acton, the words made her heart soar with joy. Oh, Lord, was she ever losing it.

She let out another long sigh, then reached for Linus. "Forgive me, Acton. I didn't mean to light into you like this. It was silly of me. And anyway, I came here to help you with Grizabella."

"You look tired. Sit down and relax for a few minutes. I'll hold Linus. Looks like he's asleep right now, anyway."

She glanced around the cozy room, with its tongue-and-groove walls, linoleum floors and multi-paned windows. A couch and armchair covered in a dark burgundy and brown patterned fabric were positioned along the outer wall, while directly across, two brown swivel rockers were separated by a wooden-tray floor lamp. The coffee table in front of the couch was cluttered with two coffee mugs and a glass filled with crushed ice and soda. Apparently he'd been eating a sandwich before she'd arrived. The crust of the bread was still lying on a paper towel.

"Sorry about the mess," he said. "I haven't had much time to clean."

"Don't apologize," she told him. "Your house looks lived in and that makes it comfortable."

She took a seat on the end of the couch and Acton joined her at the opposite end. As she watched him settle Linus comfortably against his chest, Stephanie was struck by how natural he looked with the baby in his arms. Whether he realized it or not, he was going to be a wonderful father someday—to some other woman's children. The mental image disturbed her far more than it should have.

He turned his head slightly and looked at her. "To be honest, Stephanie, I felt a bit guilty about asking you over this evening. You're so busy with the baby and work. But Grizabella has gone rogue on me and I knew you'd be the best person to help with her."

Since Stephanie hadn't heard from Acton since the night of the fund-raiser, she'd just assumed everything had gone well with Grizabella.

"Rogue?" She frowned with disbelief. "I can't believe she'd turn mean!"

"Not mean. But she's turned on me. I think she actually hates me now."

"I seriously doubt that. What did you do? Yell at her?"

"Yell? I've never talked so sweet to a female in my life." Clearly exasperated, he shook his head. "I thought bringing her home and making friends with her was going to be easy. But it's turned out to be a nightmare."

"Hmm. That is surprising. I thought she'd settle right in, too. What happened?"

"Like I told my mom, she took one look at Seymour and ran for the hills—or in this case, straight under my bed. I realize I probably shouldn't have let the dog in until Grizabella got used to her surroundings, but Seymour gets his feelings hurt if you look at him crossways. So I caved in and let him inside."

"Did the dog bark and try to chase her?"

"Not even a little. I was actually amazed that he behaved so well. But that doesn't do much good now. The only time Grizabella will poke her head out is when I set a bowl of tuna or sardines on the floor. I've already gone through a dozen or more cans!"

Stephanie laughed. "Acton, you're so funny. All you're doing is feeding her habit and teaching her to stay hidden. You have to earn her trust and show her it's okay to come out and join the land of the living."

He rolled his eyes. "Sure. That's easy for you to say. Can you show *me* how to do that?"

"I'll try. But I'd better warn you it's not something that happens in a matter of minutes. You might have to work on this for several days."

"Oh, great. That means I'll be sleeping with the smell of sardines for the next few weeks."

She chuckled. "I don't think it will be that bad."

They both fell silent after that and Stephanie was

beginning to wonder if he'd regretted asking her over when he finally asked, "So how have you been since the Valentine party?"

"Very busy. The clinic has been overrun with patients. But Linus is such a good baby. I hear these nightmare stories about babies crying with colic for the first three months of their lives. Thankfully, Linus sleeps and eats without any problems."

He gazed down at the baby. "Linus is too easygoing to get colic."

His assumption put an amused smile on her face. "How did you reach that conclusion?"

"Simple deduction. High-strung horses are usually the ones that suffer episodes of colic. I figure babies are pretty much the same." He glanced curiously at her. "Speaking of horses, did you ever work with large animals when you lived in Florida?"

"No. The vet I worked for was located in the city in a small-animal clinic. But I've always wanted the chance to work with large animals, too. Sometimes when an emergency arises, Dr. Neil will take the case. Not long ago I helped him treat a bull with an infected horn. That was fun."

Nodding, he said, "I remember. That was the day I brought Ryan and Elizabeth by the clinic—when they picked out the two cats to adopt," he said. "Carla said then that you were out back helping Dr. Neil with a bull. I figured that was something out of the ordinary."

She nodded. "It was. But who knows, Dr. Neil might decide to expand his practice someday to include large animals. Lord knows my brothers would only be too glad to construct a larger facility for the clinic."

"No doubt," he said. "Shawn and I stopped by the Crockett Café a couple of days ago and we heard plenty of talk about the new buildings going up. I think some of the old locals are expecting to see skyscrapers appear in the middle of Rambling Rose."

"I don't think anything like that is about to happen. Unless the new hotel they're planning turns out to be a high-rise building. But I'm hoping they think long and hard before they do something that extravagant. To be honest, one of the reasons I decided to move here to Rambling Rose with my brothers was because I thought small-town life would be a nice change from the city. I'd hate to see this place lose its rural charm."

"You and a lot more people," he agreed.

Wanting to change the subject, she shifted on the cushion and smiled at him. "So how have you been these past few days? Busy?"

"So busy we've hardly had time to look up. We've been building cross fence that goes for a couple of miles. Hard work, but it will be worth it. The new fence is going to make roundups much easier."

Impressed, she said, "So the Diamond D is that large?"

"By Texas standards it's a just a little patch of ground. But it's about all the four of us Donovan men can take care of." His gaze dropped to Linus and he gently traced his forefinger over the baby's cheek. After a couple moments he said, "I think I ought to tell you that my mother is concerned with the idea of me spending time with you."

Stephanie sat forward on the edge of the cushion and stared at him. "You mentioned me to your mother?"

He shook his head. "No. Someone who saw us together at the fund-raiser did."

A part of Stephanie was disappointed. If he'd been the one to tell his mother about her, it might have shown that she was becoming an important part of his life. On the other hand, it could be that he wasn't the type to discuss a girlfriend with his mother.

Stop it, Stephanie. Stop making excuses for the man. That sign around his neck doesn't read Good. It says Fun and Fickle.

Trying to shake away the sardonic voice in her head, she asked, "Why would your mother be concerned about me?"

He leveled a dry look at her. "For the same reason your brothers are concerned about me. We're not on equal footing. She thinks you'll hurt me."

"And my brothers believe you'll hurt me," she stated ruefully.

He grunted with amusement. "Yeah. Together we make a dangerous pair."

Unwittingly, she reached over and wrapped her hand around his. The contact brought his gaze around to hers, and as she studied his blue eyes, she realized she couldn't view him as something to fear. How could she fear something that made her so happy?

"It's not my plan to hurt you, Acton."

A dimple appeared in his left cheek. "I'm not planning on hurting you, either."

"So maybe our families should quit worrying about us."

"Or at least let us do the worrying," he added with a twinkle in his eyes.

His hand was warm, and for a moment she considered sliding across the cushions and snuggling up to his side. But she didn't want this evening to end with him running scared and her aching for something he wasn't ready to give.

Drawing her hand away, she focused on the messy coffee table. "Looks like you were eating when I arrived. Don't let me interrupt your meal."

Linus squirmed and Acton gently shifted the baby to his other side.

"Not at all. I'm finished. Would you like something to eat or drink? I have all kinds of cold cuts. Plus a pecan pie. I buy them from the bakery two at a time. Mom warns me that I'm going to get fat. She doesn't have a clue how much physical labor I do."

No matter how hard she tried, she couldn't imagine Acton with a roll of flab around his waistline. "No thanks. Maybe later, after we deal with Grizabella."

"I'm ready to take a go at her, if you are," he said.

Stephanie rose from the couch and picked up the diaper bag next to her feet. "Where should I put Linus's diaper bag? Will Seymour get into if I leave it on the couch?"

"With Seymour I can't make any kind of promises. Better let me put it on top of the fridge," he said.

Stephanie glanced around the room. "Speaking of Seymour, where did he get off to? He shot into the house like he couldn't wait to get in here and I've not seen him since."

"I think I know where we'll find him." Cradling Linus in one arm, he rose from the couch and jerked his head toward an open doorway on the opposite side of the room. "Follow me."

They left the living room and entered an open space where four doors intersected. Acton went directly forward and into a small kitchen decorated with red curtains, white-painted cabinets and a green Formica-and-chrome table with matching chairs. A clock in the shape of a colorful rooster hung on the wall behind the table.

"Does the rooster crow on the hour?" she asked.

He let out a good-natured groan. "No, thank goodness. I can hear Mom's real rooster all the way down here. I don't need two birds to tell me it's time to get up at four thirty in the morning."

She gazed around the cozy room. "This kitchen is adorable. I'll bet you have some memories of being here with your grandmother."

"Tons of them. She cooked all the time and my brothers and I knew if we begged hard enough she'd give us pie or something we shouldn't be eating before supper."

"Is this the way the house looked when you moved in?"

With his free hand, he placed the diaper bag on top of the fridge.

"The whole house is just like it was when Grandma Hatti moved out. It would hurt her feelings if I changed it."

"Why would you want to? It all looks fine to me. And this kitchen is just too cute."

He shrugged. "To be honest, it doesn't much matter to me how it's furnished as long as it's comfortable. But it hardly looks like a bachelor lives here."

"I imagine your grandmother appreciates you not turning it into a bachelor pad. Was this house where your grandparents always lived on the ranch?"

He nodded. "This house is more than a hundred years old. My great-grandfather built it when he first started the Diamond D. The newer house on the hill behind this one was built by my father after he and Mom got married."

"What happened to your grandfather?"

A shadow passed his face, but only for a moment. "One evening after work he sat down in his favorite chair, went to sleep and never woke up. Guess if I have a choice, that's the way I want to go."

He motioned for her to follow him and they left the kitchen and started across the hallway.

"So what do your brothers think about you moving in here?" Stephanie asked as she walked a step behind him. "Do they think they have just as much right to live here as you?"

He glanced over his shoulder at her. "They do have just as much right, but they're not interested. Shawn prefers the big house so he'll have someone cooking his meals and picking up after him. And Danny says when he gets a place of his own he wants it to be more modern."

"I see. So it didn't cause any friction between the three of you?"

As they reached another open doorway, he paused and looked at her. "No. Would something like that cause friction with your brothers?"

She let out a short laugh. "It hasn't always been easy merging four brothers from two different mothers. There's been some resentment and dissension along the way. But for the most part they get along. We all do, actually."

"Until you bring a strange cowboy into your kitchen, right?" he joked.

She pulled an impish face at him. "That's only happened once. But it could happen again," she suggested. "If the cowboy decides to help me do some more baking."

His eyebrows slowly lifted. "Maybe we ought to do the baking here. It would probably be safer."

She frowned. "You're not going to let that trio scare you away, are you?"

His lips twisted to a faint smile as he touched his forefinger to the tip of her nose. "No. In fact, I'm not going to let anything scare me away from you."

"Not even my kisses?"

His low, sexy chuckle sent a shiver down her spine.

"You get Grizabella out from under the bed and I'll show you how scared I am of your kisses."

Certain her stomach had suddenly been invaded by a thousand butterflies, she tried to make her smile provocative. "I just might hold you to that promise."

Chapter Nine

Inside Acton's bedroom, he carefully placed Linus in the middle of a queen-size bed, surrounded by pillows so there would be no chance of him rolling to the edge.

Stephanie covered the baby with a soft blanket and after making sure he was comfortable, she looked around the room. It was furnished with a varnished pine chest and dresser that matched the bed frame. Braided rugs covered part of the linoleum floor and white Priscilla curtains draped the double windows. She'd seen rooms like this in rural-living magazines, but never in person. She was struck by how homey and warm it felt.

"I'm guessing Grizabella must be under this bed," she said.

Acton nodded. "That's right. And just like I suspected, Seymour is waiting for her to come out." He nodded at the dog, who was lying at the foot of the bed, his nose resting on his paws. "When he's in the house, this is where he stays, watching for her to make a move. Would it be better if I took him outside?"

The moment he heard Acton say his name, the dog whined, but he never took his eyes off the fringe dangling at the bottom of the white bedspread.

"No," Stephanie answered. "Grizabella is going to have to get used to him. That's what caused all the problems in the first place."

Stephanie dropped to her hands and knees and peered under the bed. Grizabella was on the opposite side, hunched up next to the wall. Her one eye was as wide as a saucer as she stared fearfully at Stephanie.

"Grizabella," she said in a quiet, gentle tone. "Come here, girl. Everything is going to be all right. The dog is okay. He's not going to hurt you. And you don't want to live under the bed from now on."

The cat's ears twitched straight up, telling Stephanie that she'd recognized her voice. It was an encouraging sign, so she continued to coax the cat to her.

Finally, after several more minutes passed, Grizabella crawled over to Stephanie's hand and sniffed.

"That's right, pretty girl. You remember me, don't you?"

She rubbed the side of her face against Stephanie's fingers and after that it was short work to stroke her until she was calm enough to be picked up.

"Oh, thank God," Acton murmured under his breath so as not to excite the cat. "I thought you might use one of your magic spells to draw her out and you did."

"Grizabella has been traumatized, but she'll come out of it." She carried the cat over to Acton. "Here. You hold her now. She needs to get used to your smell and touch."

He took the cat in his arms and Stephanie thought he handled the cat with the same gentle expertise he used with Linus.

As his long fingers softly stroked the top of her head, he said, "Gosh, she's been hiding out for so long, I'd almost forgotten how pretty she is."

Unable to contain his curiosity, Seymour got up and came around to Acton. The minute he looked up at the cat and let out a whine, Grizabella arched her back and hissed. Acton managed to tighten his hold without scaring her even more.

"It's okay, girl," he said to Grizabella. "Seymour is really just a softy. He wouldn't hurt a flea if it was biting his tail."

Stephanie had to stifle a laugh. "That's not what I heard."

"Shh. She doesn't know that," Acton scolded. "Besides, his problem isn't with other animals. It's with people—namely, me."

Stephanie drew close enough to place her hand on Seymour's head, then, using a soft voice, attempted to introduce the two animals.

"I think it's working," Acton said after a few minutes. "I can feel Grizabella relaxing in my arms."

Stephanie continued to size up the two animals' behavior. "I believe you're right. The look she's giving Seymour now is more like curiosity rather than terror. And Seymour is clearly infatuated with her. He wants her to get down and play."

"I don't think she's feeling that friendly," Acton replied. "What if I take her in the kitchen and try to feed her? I still have a can of mackerel left."

"I'll go with you. Just in case of an emergency," she added.

"That doesn't sound encouraging."

Stephanie laughed at his wariness. "You're a rancher. You've been around animals all your life. You should know they're unpredictable."

"Yeah. I have scars on my body to prove just how unpredictable. I'll show them to you sometime. Just so you'll know I'm not lying."

"Uh, I believe you. For now," she added in a suggestive voice.

It was his turn to laugh and then he glanced at

Linus. "Will the baby be okay there if we both go to the kitchen?"

"Sure. He's perfectly safe. Plus I'll be just a few feet away. I can hear him if he so much as makes a peep."

"Good. Then, let's take this pair to the kitchen and give it a try."

Nearly a half hour later, the two animals had come to a truce and Seymour was lying on his belly patiently watching Grizabella eat the last of her mackerel. With only a few feet between the cat and dog and neither trying to make a dash for it, Stephanie and Acton decided a beautiful friendship was beginning to bud between the two.

"I thought they might become friends," she stated happily as she sat at the table, sipping coffee that Acton had made for her. "But I never believed it would happen this quickly. I thought I might have to make several trips over here to help get them acquainted."

Acton snapped his fingers. "Shoot. Now I'll have to think up another excuse to get you here again."

Stephanie leveled a wry look at him. "Why don't you just ask? Wouldn't that be simpler?"

A sheepish grin slanted his lips. "Yeah, I guess it would. Can you come over Saturday? I promised Ryan and Elizabeth that I'd take them to the park in town. But I was thinking we could have a little picnic here. I have an outdoor fireplace in the backyard.

I can build a fire and let the kids roast wieners and marshmallows. And if it's warm enough, we can walk them down to the pond. What do you think?"

Stephanie didn't know what to think. Being invited to another family outing with the kids was the last thing she'd expected from him.

"I realize it probably sounds boring to you," he went on. "But Elizabeth and Ryan have been hounding me about this for the past month and they would love your company. So would I."

For a man who was gun-shy of love and marriage, he was hardly acting like a playboy. Dayna and Sheri had both gossiped to her about a few of the women he'd dated during the past few years, and according to Stephanie's coworkers, Acton had dropped each woman after a brief fling. She didn't want to believe her friends were making up gossip, but when Stephanie was with him, he seemed anything but a womanizer. Was she stupid to think he might've put his roaming ways behind him? Or that he might not have been that much of a playboy in the first place?

Stephanie wasn't going to worry about answering that question. Risky or not, she wanted to be with the man.

"I think it sounds lovely, Acton. I can bring some things for the picnic. And don't worry, I'll get them from the deli instead of trying to make them," she said with a laugh.

She was surprised at the happy look that spread

over his face. It very nearly matched the joy that was bubbling over inside of her. It didn't matter if they had three children as chaperones. Acton wanted to spend time with her and in the end that's all that really mattered.

Chuckling, he said, "Don't worry about bringing any food. Having you and Linus here is what's important to me."

Just as she started to make a reply, Linus let out a whimper and Stephanie quickly rose to her feet and grabbed the diaper bag off the fridge.

"Linus calls. He's probably wet and hungry," she said.

To her surprise, Acton followed her into the bedroom, where they sat down on opposite sides of the bed.

"Why don't you let me change him?" he offered. "I know how to do it. I changed plenty of Elizabeth's and Ryan's diapers."

She cast him a doubtful glance. "That's hard to believe. You were still in your teens when those two were born. You were probably running around with your friends, playing sports and riding horses or something."

"True, I was doing all those things. But I still had time for my niece and nephew. And teenagers make good babysitters. At least, Gina always trusted me. She said Shawn didn't have the patience for kids and Danny wouldn't know which end of a bottle went into the baby's mouth. She said I had finesse with babies," he said proudly.

Stephanie laughed. "Like I have with animals?"

"Exactly."

She pulled a diaper out of the bag and handed it to him. "Then I would think you'd have some children of your own by now."

Shooting her a perplexed look, he reached for Linus. "I'm only twenty-five. I have lots of time to have babies. Besides, I told you the kind of women I've dated in the past. None of them were what I'd consider mother material."

Just like none of the men she'd dated were husband or father material, Stephanie thought dismally.

He removed Linus's diaper and rolled it up tightly. "Do you use wipes on him?"

Stephanie handed him a disposable wipe and a tube of protective ointment. "This seems to keep him from getting diaper rash. And thankfully, the women at the day care are wonderful about keeping him changed and dry."

He wiped the baby's bottom, then smeared a thin glaze of ointment onto his skin. All the while Linus kicked and cooed like he was enjoying every second of Acton's attention.

"There. He's all fixed and ready to go for another round." He propped the baby against his shoulder and gently rubbed his back. "Do you think he's hungry?"

"Maybe. Since he's not yelling for a bottle yet, I

was thinking I really should be going home, Acton. It's getting late and my brothers have no idea where I am."

He arched an eyebrow at her. "I've never heard you express any concerns about your brothers keeping up with your whereabouts. I'm thinking you might be using them as an excuse to leave. Right?"

She smiled sheepishly. "Okay. I confess. I'm guilty. That was just an excuse."

"Good. Because I'd really like for you to stay a little longer. Will you?"

How could she tell him no? Not when being with him felt so good.

"All right," she said, relenting to the persuasiveness of his tempting smile. "For a while longer, anyway."

Their gazes locked and Stephanie's heart thumped with anticipation. The light from the lamp behind him lit the blond curls scattered across his forehead to a rich, golden hue. Couple that with his tanned skin and sky-blue eyes, and his face was like a Technicolor dream. Almost too vibrant to be real.

"I did promise to kiss you if you got Grizabella to leave her hiding place under the bed," he murmured. "I need the chance to pay up."

Her heart began to pound, and as he leaned across the bed toward her, her breath stalled in her throat. When his face was inches from hers, she wet her lips in anticipation… And then Linus let out a frustrated cry, shattering the tense connection between them.

"On second thought, I guess he's hungry," she said, her voice husky. "Here's your chance to feed him."

For a moment the look on his face made her think he was going to ignore the baby's cries and kiss her anyway. But then he suddenly cleared his throat and reached for Linus and with a pang of regret, Stephanie realized the chance to feel his lips pressed to hers was over.

Twenty minutes later, the baby was full of formula and sound asleep. Acton laid him on the floor, atop an armchair cushion, and covered him with a blanket, then looked across to Stephanie. She'd taken off her ankle boots and now her bare feet were curled beneath her.

She looked tired, but beautiful, and though he should've felt guilty about keeping her here, he didn't. For the past three days, he'd been fighting an inner battle. One minute he'd convinced himself that he was walking down a losing path to think Stephanie could be more than a temporary girlfriend. And then there'd been moments where he hadn't given a damn about her money or social status.

"Well, the Texas sandman has done a number on him," Acton said. "He ought to sleep for a while."

"Texas sandman? Is that what you call him?"

Smiling, he eased down next to her on the couch and crossed his ankles out in front of him. "Mom used to sing that lullaby to us kids. It's all about the Texas sandman coming to visit and he puts you on a palomino pony with a saddle made of moonbeams and you ride over the Milky Way, beneath a blanket of stars."

"Oh, it sounds charming. Can you sing it?"

The only time Acton sang was in the shower, or on the back of a horse. Definitely not to a girl. "I don't remember exactly how the words go. Besides, you wouldn't want to hear me sing. But I can hum the melody for you. If you'd like."

She turned eagerly toward him. "I'd love it."

Taking her hand, he clasped it between his and began to hum the soft melody that he'd heard from the time he was a little boy. The enchanted look that came over her face had Acton feeling as though he was floating among those moonbeams. Or was it the touch of her hand that had sent him flying over the Milky Way?

Once he finished humming, she said softly, "That's beautiful, Acton. Really."

"Not as beautiful as you," he murmured.

Her smile was wobbly and he wondered if her heart could possibly be beating as wildly as his. It was thumping hard against his rib cage, and each beat begged him to pull her close, to kiss her until the room around them disappeared and they were cloaked in dark velvet.

Lifting his hand to her face, he stroked his fingertips gently across her forehead. "I don't have to go outside to see the stars. They're right here in your eyes."

"Isn't that kind of cheesy?" she asked.

"Probably. But I love cheese. Don't you?"

She chuckled. "All kinds."

Their gazes locked and her blue eyes conveyed a need that came close to stealing his breath. His hands cradled her face and he thought how touching her skin was like stroking satin. "Stephanie, you're so beautiful and special. All I want is to be close to you."

"Close. Yes, that's all I want, too."

His heart racing, he bent his head and gently touched his lips to hers. She responded instantly by slipping her arms around his neck and pressing her body against his.

Her eager reaction was all it took for Acton to deepen the kiss, and as he wrapped his arms around her, he was certain he'd never felt anything so delicate and warm and utterly precious.

Her lips were unbelievably soft and giving, and in a matter of seconds he was lost, his senses swirling faster and faster. Heat shot through his body like a bolt of lightning, and when her hands began to move up and down his arms, the sensation was like a pair of torches burning all the way through to his bones.

Hanging onto his control by a flimsy thread, he tried to rein it in. But before he could get a grip, her mouth opened and the tip of her tongue boldly pushed against his teeth. The intimate request broke the last of his restraint and he gladly let her inside. When their tongues began a slow dance, the contact caused fire to spread low in his loins.

For days now he'd thought of little more than kissing her again. Really kissing her. Yet now that he had her in his arms, he realized that kissing wasn't nearly enough to ease the ache inside him. And from the hungry way her mouth was clinging to his, it wasn't enough for her.

Pushed by the certainty, he cupped a hand around one breast and rubbed his thumb against the center. Her response was a tiny moan from deep in her throat, and the sound of her pleasure thrilled him. The idea that she could want him, even a fraction of how much he wanted her, was enough to rattle his senses. But his feelings didn't stop with the physical. No, his emotions were being sucked along, too, and the mixture was like a giant tidal wave washing over him, tugging him back and forth like a dangerous undercurrent.

The kiss went on for so long that Acton's lungs began to scream for a fresh load of oxygen. Yet the thought of deserting her lips, even for the sake of breathing, was torturous. And then her hands found their way beneath his T-shirt and pushed their way upward until her palms were lying flat against his chest.

The contact sent his head reeling even more and he was forced to tear his lips from hers and suck in a long, raspy breath.

"Stephanie, do you still think I don't want to kiss you?"

She pressed kisses over his chin and along his jaw until her lips hovered near his ear. "You've come close to convincing me that you do. But I think you need to show me more," she whispered.

She raked her fingers through his hair and he brought his lips back to hers. This time their mouths fused together in a kiss so deep and hot that the flames shot straight to his brain, then licked their way downward until the very soles of his feet were burning.

When their bodies listed to one side, he didn't try to stop the downward slide. By the time she was lying flat against the couch, all he wanted was to stretch out beside her, feel the whole length of her against him.

Without breaking the kiss, he fumbled with the buttons of her blouse. Once the fabric parted enough to reveal the top of one breast, he gently traced his fingertips over her flesh, then dipped them beneath the lacy cup of her bra.

The moment they came in contact with her nipple, a needy moan vibrated deep in her throat. Spurred by the sound, Acton teased the hard bud until the urge to taste it became too much to bear.

Lowering his head, he pulled the lace downward until the rosy pink nipple came into view.

With her hands on the back of his head, she guided his mouth to the heated point. Using his tongue, Acton circled the flesh, then drew it between his teeth. As he did, he felt Stephanie's fingers curling into his scalp and her leg slipping over his.

Desperate to explore more of her, he finished with the buttons on her shirt and pushed the tails away to expose her flat belly. His fingers slipped over the flesh and as he savored the incredible smoothness, his nostrils pulled in the fresh, flowery scent that clung to her clothes and skin.

The thought suddenly struck him that if he stayed on the couch all night with her wrapped in his arms, it wouldn't be long enough. If his lips could kiss hers a thousand times over and over, it would only whet his appetite for more. This desire he felt for her wasn't a one-and-done thing. It went far deeper than that and the realization caused him to lift his head and stare wondrously down at her.

"What's wrong, Acton?"

The blue pools of her eyes were filled with confusion and as Acton gazed into them, he was suddenly reminded of the night of the Valentine's party. He'd run from her kisses that night, because even then he'd recognized that what he was feeling wasn't like anything he'd experienced before. And now he knew for certain that whatever was growing between them was more than hot chemistry.

"Nothing is wrong," he murmured, then leaned slightly and pressed a kiss to her damp forehead. "You…this—it all feels wonderful to me. And I don't want it to stop. I want to make love to you, Stephanie. Right here. Right now."

"And what would be wrong with that?"

"Nothing. If I was sure that's what you really wanted. That you wouldn't regret it later."

Her eyebrows puckered together. "How do you know I'm not sure?"

"Because this—whatever it is—has happened between us rather quickly. You haven't had that much time to think about who I am and how I might fit in your life."

Her eyes suddenly filled with dark shadows, as she studied his face. "And you need time to figure out who I am and where I might fit in your life?"

He nodded, then cupped his hand around her chin and said, "That's what I'm thinking. But I get the feeling you believe I'm making excuses."

Sighing, she pushed herself to a sitting position, and with trembling fingers adjusted her bra and began to button her shirt. "No. I'm thinking you're making much more sense than me. I, uh, have always had a problem of following my feelings and worrying about the consequences later."

The sadness he saw on her face twisted something deep in his heart and Acton realized that no matter what happened in the future, he never wanted to cause Stephanie a moment of pain.

Leaning his head close to hers, he placed a kiss on her cheekbone. "Stephanie, I don't want to be like those guys who took advantage of your sweet, giving heart. When you make love to me—and I hope you do—I want it to be special. I want you to give yourself to me because deep down you know that you can trust me."

Moisture suddenly sprang to her eyes and threatened to spill onto her cheeks. The sight was like a hand squeezing his heart.

"I want it to be like that, too, Acton. Really."

A wry smile slanted his lips. "Then why are you crying?"

She shook her head. "Because I never expected to hear you say something like that to me."

His fingertips traced light circles on her cheek. "To be honest, Steph, I didn't know I could say that kind of thing to a woman. You're a first," he said wryly.

With a little moan, she hugged his neck, then before the sparks had a chance to start flying again, she rose to her feet and straightened her clothing.

"I think I'd better be going on home, Acton. It's getting late and I have to be up early."

In spite of all that talk about giving her time, he didn't want her to go. And the realization had him wondering what it would be like if they were married and she and Linus lived here with him. Instead of seeing her out to her car, he'd be taking her by the hand and leading her to the bedroom. Their bedroom. He'd wake up with her face on the pillow next to his. With her sitting across from him at the breakfast table. Maybe the monotony of married life wasn't what his brothers wanted for themselves, but Acton was beginning to think he could darned sure get used to it.

That is, as long as the woman at his side was Stephanie.

With that impossible dream swirling around in his head, Acton rose from the couch. "I'll carry Linus out to the car for you."

Chapter Ten

Saturday morning turned out to be one of those late February days in Texas that felt more like a day in May. As Stephanie carried Linus and his packed-to-the-brim diaper bag out to the car, the sun was shining warmly with just enough breeze to move the leaves on the live oaks.

During the drive to Acton's, the memory of her last visit to his house made a haunting circle through her head. Had he been thinking about her and how close they'd come to making love? The same way she'd been thinking about it? Every detail of those moments she'd spent in his arms were still achingly vivid and she couldn't wait to see him again, touch him again, even if it had to be in an innocent way.

When she arrived twenty minutes later, Elizabeth and Ryan were waiting for her at the front-yard gate. Chattering with excitement, both children greeted her with enthusiastic hugs, then promptly began to argue over which one of them could carry Linus's diaper bag into the house.

Thankfully, Acton appeared to remind the pair to behave or run the risk of being confined to the house for the rest of their stay. Which would've been a shame considering the nice weather.

As it turned out, it was warm enough for Stephanie to take Linus to the patio and join in on the fun of roasting wieners and marshmallows for their lunch.

After the meal, the five of them left the backyard and walked down a well-trodden path to a large pond partially shaded by a stand of willows. While she and Acton watched, the kids threw food to the fish, a task that kept them busy for a good half hour.

Once they walked back to the house, Acton got out a board game for the children and set it up on the coffee table in the living room. The four of them played, until an argument ensued over Elizabeth's claim that Ryan was cheating. Acton decided the best way to settle the issue was to end the game and turn on the television.

While the two kids became absorbed in a movie about a little boy searching for his lost dog, Stephanie and Acton sat on the couch and talked about their own childhoods.

"Did you always like horses and ranches?" she asked him. "Or was it something you simply fell into because you were born to a ranching family?"

"True, I was born into it. But I never wanted to be anything but a cowboy. Same for Shawn. In fact, when we were teenagers the two of us used to dream that one day we'd be rodeo stars and wear big shiny world-championship buckles." He grunted with self-directed humor. "We tried, but someone else got the buckles."

Intrigued, Stephanie asked, "What event did you do?"

"We both rode saddle broncs. It takes a lot of balance and finesse to be good at it and of the two of us, Shawn was better. But neither of us was championship material," he told her, then shrugged. "We both decided ranching was the safest way to make a living."

She shook her head with amazement. "I can't imagine getting on a bucking horse. Did you ever fall off and get stomped or kicked?"

He chuckled. "Plenty of times. It goes with the sport."

"And what did your parents say about you and your brother participating in such a dangerous event?"

"Surprisingly, it was Dad who disapproved. He

didn't forbid us to ride broncs, but he was hardly thrilled about the idea. Mom has always been the adventurous sort, far more than Dad, so she was all for it. She'd be in the stands watching, yelling and clapping us on."

Acton's mother hadn't worried about him riding a bucking horse, but she was concerned about him spending time with Stephanie. On first thought, the idea was ludicrous. The dangerous sport could have left Acton's body mangled. But sometimes a physical injury wasn't nearly as devastating as a crushed and hopeless spirit. And from Faye Donovan's viewpoint, she'd probably rather see her son wearing a cast on his arm instead of watching him try to piece a broken heart back together.

"It's nice to have a parent in your corner, rooting you on," she said wistfully.

Curiosity was in his eyes as he studied her face. "You say that as if you don't always get along well with your parents."

"Oh, no. I'm close to both of them," she quickly corrected him. "I honestly can't think of any major arguments I've had with Dad or Mother. But..." She paused then let out a sigh. "I'll be honest, with eight of us kids, sometimes I felt left out. Dad has always been driven with his work. He's in the gaming business. Video games, I should say."

"So that's how he acquired his wealth? Or did he inherit the money from his father?"

Stephanie practically cringed at the question. "The subject of Dad's father isn't something we talk about in the family. It's a pretty sore subject. You see, Dad's father, Julius Fortune, would never acknowledge David as his son. So, no, Dad's money came from years of hard work and determination."

Acton was clearly confused. "He wouldn't acknowledge his own son? Damn, that's tough."

Stephanie nodded. "Well, you see, Dad was the result of one of Julius's many affairs. To acknowledge him would've been the same as owning up to his sins."

Rubbing a thoughtful hand against his jaw, he looked over at Elizabeth and Ryan stretched out on the floor, both entranced by the lost dog trotting across the television screen. Then his gaze slipped over to Linus, who was sound asleep on the chair cushion. Was he thinking like Stephanie? That neither parent seemed to want the adorable baby? The idea was heartbreaking.

"I can't imagine my own father not wanting me or what that would do to a man's psyche," he said.

"It's a painful wound that Dad has tried to bury away and not talk about, but I figure it's colored the way he's raised us eight children."

His lips took on a wry slant. "Mom mentioned that she'd read about the Fortunes in Austin having family troubles. Something about their house burning and a son being injured. Are those your relatives?"

Grimacing, she nodded. "Yes. Although we don't really associate with them. Jerome Fortune, who goes by the name of Gerald Robinson, is my father's half-brother. From what I can gather, he's been just as much of a tomcat as their father Julius. Trust me, Acton, my father and my family aren't like the Austin Fortunes. I mean, we're far from perfect, but we certainly have not had the kind of drama that's gone on with the Fortune Robinsons. Is that why your mother is worried about you? She thinks all of us Fortunes are dysfunctional?"

Smiling now, Acton reached over and squeezed her hand. "She doesn't know you, Stephanie. Not yet. But when she does, she's going to love you."

Was he saying he intended to introduce her to his parents? She wasn't about to ask him. Not now. But the thought was enough to put a spark of hope in her heart.

It was nearing five o'clock that evening, when Gina arrived to pick up the children. As soon as Acton's sister entered the house, she promptly gave Stephanie a big hug, then went straight to where Linus was lying on the cushion.

"I was so hoping he would be here with you," Gina exclaimed as she bent over the baby. "Acton has told me how cute he is and he wasn't exaggerating. Look at that hair. And his eyes are so bright. You must be totally in love with him."

"I'm crazy in love with Linus." *Along with your brother.* The added thought came out of nowhere, shocking Stephanie with its connotations. Had she already fallen in love with Acton? Oh, Lord, if that was the case, then it was far too late to be worrying whether he was that one good man she'd been hoping to come into her life. Her fate was already sealed.

Gina glanced over her shoulder at Stephanie. "May I hold him?" she asked.

"Of course," Stephanie told her. "Linus loves being held."

Gina picked up the baby and, gently rocking him in her arms, began to meander slowly around the room.

After watching his sister for a moment, Acton gave Stephanie a conspiring wink. "Better be careful, sis," he warned Gina. "Holding Linus might put you in the mood to have another baby."

Laughing coyly, Gina said, "Who knows, maybe it will. Jack would definitely like to be a daddy again."

Picking up on the conversation, Elizabeth walked over and tugged on the leg of her mother's jeans. "Are we gonna take Linus home with us, Mommy?"

"No, honey. Linus belongs with Stephanie."

"But couldn't we keep him for a little while, then give him back?" the girl asked hopefully.

"It doesn't work that way, Lizzie," Gina told her daughter. "You wouldn't want me to give you away for a little while, would you?"

Tilting her head to one side, Elizabeth pondered her mother's question. "Well, if you gave me to Uncle Acton it would be okay. He lets us do fun stuff that you don't let us do."

Gina shot her brother a dry look. "Thanks, Acton, for making me look like a meanie."

Grinning, Acton held up his hands in an innocent gesture. "I'm just letting them be kids."

"Yeah, well, just wait 'til you have some of your own. It's going to be my chance for payback."

He didn't have a reply for that and Stephanie wondered what he was thinking. That it would be years and years before a child called him Daddy? If so, that meant she and Linus could hardly hope for him to make them a family of three.

You're putting the cart before the horse, Stephanie. You have no idea how long Linus will be your little baby, much less if Acton will ever hear wedding bells.

Stephanie tried to shake off the pessimistic voice in her head while across the room, Gina replaced Linus on the chair cushion and informed Elizabeth and Ryan it was time for them to go.

Once the children had collected their backpacks, Acton rose from the couch. "I'll walk out with you and the kids," he said to Gina.

Before they went out the door, Elizabeth and Ryan came over to the couch and gave Stephanie goodbye hugs.

"Will you come to our house sometime?" Ryan asked. "We want you to see Roscoe and Rosie."

"Yeah!" Elizabeth seconded. "The cats are happy 'cause Mommy lets them sleep on the foot of our beds. Only because their hair doesn't come out."

"She means as long as Roscoe and Rosie don't shed they get to sleep on the bed," Ryan drolly explained.

The girl wrinkled her nose at her brother. "That's just what I said, smarty!"

Groaning, Gina put a hand on each child's shoulder and ushered them toward the door. "Okay, kids, let's go before you give Stephanie a headache."

Stephanie waved a goodbye to the three of them and Acton followed his relatives out the door.

Less than two minutes later, she heard Gina's car drive away.

By the time Acton returned from outside, her heart was beating with anticipation. This would be the first time they'd been alone together since the night she'd helped him with Grizabella. Had he forgotten the kisses they'd shared? How close they'd come to making love? All day today he hadn't so much as hinted at what had occurred between them and Stephanie was beginning to wonder if he'd decided forgetting would be best for both of them.

"Well, they're on their way," Acton said. "The kids wanted me to tell you they had a good time."

Stephanie's nerves were suddenly so overwrought

that she jumped to her feet. "I'm, uh, glad. I really enjoyed them, too."

Picking up on her anxiousness, he asked, "What's wrong? You look like Grizabella when she first laid eyes on Seymour."

Her short laugh had a silly, breathless sound to it. "Nothing is wrong. I thought I'd go clean up your kitchen."

"I've already thrown the paper cups and plates in the garbage, so there's nothing to clean." A coy smile was on his face as he walked over and sandwiched one of her hands between the two of his. "And now that it's quiet and we're alone, I have something to show you."

Puzzled, she asked, "To show me? Where is this something? Should I bring Linus?"

After switching off the television, he walked over and collected Linus. "I'll bring Linus," he said. "You follow me."

They left the living room, but rather than head to the kitchen, he made an abrupt left, toward his bedroom. Throughout the day she'd noticed the door had remained closed and she'd assumed it was to keep the children from prowling though his personal belongings. Now she wondered if he was hiding something.

"Have you trapped a monster in here and it's going to jump out at us?" she teased. "I know it can't be Seymour and Grizabella. They're cuddled up together on a rug in the living room."

"Hmm. What a nasty imagination you have," he replied.

"I grew up with four brothers. I know what kind of tricks you guys like to play on us unsuspecting females."

Chuckling, he opened the door and gestured for her to precede him into the room.

The shades behind the white Priscilla curtains were closed, blocking out most of the late-afternoon sunlight to leave dusky shadows around the room.

Acton walked over to the nightstand and switched on a small lamp. A circle of soft light spread over the room and Stephanie's attention was immediately drawn to the dresser, where a blue printed vase held a bouquet of pink rosebuds. The sight of the flowers was surprising enough, but then she spotted the cradle near the foot of the bed and couldn't contain her loud gasp.

"Oh, my! A cradle! A real wooden cradle!" She rushed over to the small baby bed and ran her fingers over the smooth grains of the maple wood. Years of use had given it a soft patina and Stephanie could only wonder how many babies had once slept in it, and how many mothers had rocked their loved ones. "Where did you get this? It's obviously an antique, so I hate to think what you paid for it!"

Amazed, Stephanie looked over at him for an explanation and he came to stand next to her.

"I could tell you that I paid a small fortune for

it, just to impress you," he said. "But that would be lying. I didn't pay a cent. I brought it down from the attic. It's the cradle my mother used for all of us kids. My grandfather made it years ago, before his children were born."

Overwhelmed, her hand crept up to cover her open mouth. "And you want Linus to use it?"

"That's why I got it out of storage. While you're here with me, Linus needs a bed of his own," he answered, then asked, "Would you like for me to put him in it? Or would you rather do it?"

He'd been a busy man, Stephanie thought, as she noticed the inside of the cradle was all ready to use with a thick mattress made up neatly with pale yellow linens. The fact that Acton had gone to so much trouble, not only for her, but also for her baby, was enough to bring tears to her eyes.

"Oh, you put him in it, Acton, please," she said huskily.

He placed Linus in the bed and after tucking the cover around him, gently pushed the rocker into motion.

Linus gave them a drooling grin and waved his arms. His reaction caused both Stephanie and Acton to laugh.

"He likes it," Acton said in a hushed voice. "Thank goodness. It was going to be pretty disappointing if the thing had made him cry."

Still overwhelmed, Stephanie looked up to Acton

to see he was smiling down at Linus. "I can't believe you went to all this trouble, Acton. And why didn't you show it to me earlier?"

Shaking his head, he said, "It isn't trouble to do something for someone you care about. And I wanted to share this with you and only you."

She walked over to the dresser and touched a finger to one of the rosebuds. "I haven't noticed fresh flowers in your house before. Are these for Linus, too?"

Two long strides put him at her side. "No. I had someone else in mind when I got those." He rested his hands on the tops of her shoulders and began to gently knead them. "Someone with golden red hair and the prettiest blue eyes I've ever looked into."

Turning toward him, she slipped her arms around his waist and tilted her head back in order to look up at him.

"Acton, you…" She paused and tried to swallow the ball of emotion clogging her throat. "You didn't have to do these things to make me want you more."

His lips took on a wry twist as the back of his fingers grazed her cheek. "Is that what you think I'm doing? Trying to win your favors?"

Her cheeks suddenly flamed with heat. "No. I, uh, I guess it's hard for me to believe that you want to give to me instead of take."

Groaning, he framed her face with both hands, then bent his head and placed a soft kiss on her lips.

"You better believe it, Stephanie. Because I do want to give to you. Not riches—because I'm not a rich man. But I can give you me—if that's enough."

"Oh, Acton. You're all I want. Truly."

Tightening her hold on his waist, she pressed against him and he immediately brought his lips back down to hers.

Chapter Eleven

Acton's kiss was tender, evoking an emotion in Stephanie that filled her heart to overflowing. Her mouth and her hands clung to him, while everything inside her begged her to never let him go.

He continued to kiss her in that same gentle manner until the warm contact ignited a bright flame. Before Stephanie realized it, their mouths were fused together in a kiss so hot she was sure that every inch of her body was on fire.

When the need for oxygen finally tore them apart, they were both breathing hard, staring at each other with raw hunger.

"Acton, don't turn away from me. Not now," she whispered.

His hands came up to cradle her face. "I have no intentions of turning away. As long as I know this is what you want."

"Let me show how much," she whispered, her hands already reaching for the snaps on his Western shirt.

With very little effort, the fasteners popped apart and she pushed aside the wash-worn denim. His muscled chest was wide and warm, and so inviting that she couldn't stop herself from leaning forward and placing her lips on the smooth flesh.

He tasted salty and oh, so masculine, and as she moved her open mouth against his skin, she pulled the erotic scent of him deep into her nostrils.

"Stephanie." Her name came out on a whisper as his fingers thrust into her hair and slid against her scalp until they were loosely cradling the back of her head. "This is… You're torturing me."

Making slow circles across his chest, she came to one flat brown nipple and licked at it with her tongue. The contact pulled an anguished groan from his throat and she smiled against him.

"Do you want me to stop?" she asked, her voice thick and husky.

"No! I mean…yes! If you keep doing this, it's all going to end…before it ever begins," he said tightly.

Tilting her head back, she looked up to see his

features were strained, as though he was fighting to stay in control. The idea that she was arousing him to such heights amazed her, and filled her with the confidence to be the woman she'd always wanted to be. The kind of woman who could take a man's love and boldly give her all back to him.

"Then let me undress you." Even as she murmured the suggestion, she was pushing the shirt off his shoulders and down his arms until the sleeves stuck at his wrists. She fumbled with the cuffs, until the snaps came loose and she was able to pull the shirt over his hands and toss it to the floor.

"It's my turn now," he said, reaching for the hem of her magenta-colored sweater.

She held up her arms and he pulled the garment over her head, then tossed it backward in the direction of where his shirt had landed. With the glow of the lamp lighting her skin, he made a slow survey of the image she made in a lacy black bra and black skinny jeans.

Stephanie had always kept herself slim and fit, but she could hardly be called anything close to curvy or voluptuous. Now as Acton's gaze swept over her, she wondered what was going on in his head. Was she a disappointment to him?

Finally, he whispered, "You look incredible."

Stunned that such a word had come out of his mouth, her head swung back and forth. "I'm glad there's not much light in here. Otherwise, you'd see

I'm far from incredible. But I won't mind at all if you say it again."

His hands settled lightly on her shoulders, their warmth promising pleasures to come. "Oh, Stephanie, no matter what's happened in your past, you're wrong to doubt yourself."

The tenderness in his voice tightened her throat and filled her chest with a heavy ache of longing. "I want to be beautiful—for you, Acton."

"Honey, if you were any more beautiful I couldn't stand it," he murmured as his fingers slipped beneath the straps of her bra and slowly eased them off her shoulders. Slowly, the lace fell away from her breasts and he bent his head to brush his lips across one nipple and then the other.

The sensation was so light and teasing it had her aching for more. But just as she snared a hold on the back of his neck to anchor his head to her breasts, he suddenly stepped back and reached for the zipper on her jeans.

His eyes glittering, he said, "You have too many clothes on."

Her head swimming, all she could think about was having his hands on her flesh, his mouth on hers, and their bodies connected in the most basic way.

"So do you," she told him, her voice little more than a breathy whisper. "And I think we should do something about it. Don't you?"

His response was to ease her backward until her

upper body was lying across the bed and her legs were dangling against the mattress. Then his hands were on her jeans, easing them down her legs until the fabric bunched around her ankle boots.

He rapidly dealt with the footwear, then slipped the jeans and a pair of black panties over her feet. Once the garments had fallen to the floor, he turned his attention to removing the last of his clothing.

From her place on the bed, Stephanie watched through half-closed eyes as he tugged off his cowboy boots, then tossed his jeans and a pair of navy blue boxers to the floor behind him.

She'd expected him to look lean and fit, but she'd not been prepared for the wide expanse of his shoulders, the narrowness of his waist, or the hard, rigid indentions of his abdomen. His legs were long and corded with heavy muscle, as were his arms, and she didn't have to wonder if he was a physically powerful man. It was all there for her to see. Including his bold erection.

The sight of his naked body was all it took to create an ache deep in her feminine core and she realized she had never wanted any man as much as she wanted Acton at this very moment.

Turning toward her, he stepped between her legs and trailed his fingers down both of her thighs, then back up to the lower portion of her belly.

Groaning, she smiled at him. "Those hands of yours should come with a danger warning."

Growling with pleasure, he looped lazy circles over her skin, all the while moving downward until he reached the juncture between her thighs. By the time his finger slipped inside her, she was frantically arching her hips upward, searching for the pleasure only he could give her.

Over and over he stroked her, until she reached up to curl a hand at the back of his neck and yank him down to her for a kiss. His tongue instantly found its way between her teeth and he stroked the inside of her mouth with the same tormenting rhythm his finger was making in the heated folds of her womanhood.

The attack on her senses was too much for Stephanie to take and in a matter of seconds, she felt herself morphing into a beautiful bird, soaring into the wind and flying high above the clouds.

When she finally glided back to earth, Acton's face was hovered above hers and everything she'd ever wanted was mirrored in his blue eyes.

Her throat thick, she whispered, "You're not playing fair, Acton."

A smug smile tilted the corners of his lips. "All I want is to please you, Stephanie."

"Then please me more, Acton, and more," she begged.

He eased away from her and stood up, reaching for the nightstand. "I think I'd better find some protection."

"Wait!" The word popped before she could stop it and he looked at her with confusion.

"I'm sorry, Acton. That didn't come out right. I just wanted to say that I'm on the Pill. So if you're concerned about pregnancy…don't worry." Just to keep her periods regular, she could've told him. But there was no need for that much explanation. He didn't need to know it had been ages since she'd had sex.

The tense look on his face relaxed and then a smile brightened his face in the dimly lit room. "Oh. Okay. But still, I want to make sure we're both protected."

He glanced over to where Linus was lying quietly in his cradle. "No need to worry about Linus. He's already gone to sleep."

Stephanie held her arms invitingly up to him and he gladly joined her on the bed, then scooped her into his arms.

When he found her mouth, she wrapped her arms around him, drawing her body tightly to his. He was all heat and hard muscle and in a matter of seconds she was lost in a cyclone of swirling sensations.

Somewhere in the back of her mind, she sensed his hands were cupping her breasts, roaming across her back, down her legs, then back up to her rounded bottom. Each spot his fingers touched left her skin burning and tingling with pleasure and she knew with certainty that she could never get enough of this. Of him.

Once his hands had made a tantalizing tour of her body, he turned his attention to her breasts, kissing and nipping the nipples until they were rigid and throbbing. By the time, he finally rolled her to her back and poised himself above her, quickly sheathing himself in the condom he'd taken from the bedside table, Stephanie's insides were clawing and screaming to be connected to him. Yet when he did finally enter her, she wasn't prepared for the shock of pleasure that lanced through her like a white-hot arrow. It was breathtaking and all-consuming, and for the space of a heartbeat, she was too stunned to move or speak.

And then from somewhere above her, she heard him groan her name and the sound shattered her momentary paralysis.

"Acton," she murmured, her voice full of anguished need. "Make love to me. Please make love to me."

"Yes, sweet Stephanie. Oh, yes."

Bracing his weight with his hands on either side of her head, he began to move in a slow, enticing rhythm that led her brain straight into a mindless pool of desire. Robbed of all sensibility, her body took over and she met each thrust of his hips with reckless abandon.

Then just when she was thinking she could go on

making love to him forever, she felt his pace quicken and his breathing grow harsh. Gripping his back, she tried to hang on, to slow the runaway freight train that was carrying them faster and faster toward their ultimate destination.

But she couldn't stop it. With one final thrust, the room around her began to whirl and she was suddenly lost, riding a wave of bliss that was taking her all the way to the moon and back.

As soon as Acton had pulled Stephanie's sweater over her head and she'd stood there before him with such a look of self-doubt on her face, he'd known he was in deep trouble.

At that moment, he'd wanted to do more than have sex with Stephanie—he'd wanted to make love to her. Real love. The kind that connected a man and a woman together until the last breaths of their lives.

And now as she was lying curled up beside him in the middle of the bed, the urge to protect her, to keep her safely by his side, had grown to enormous proportions. How had this happened? Why had he allowed it to happen?

Love isn't something you can control, Acton. It's something that hits you even when you think you don't want it, or need it. So now, good or bad, you'll just have to learn to live with it.

"It's not been dark for very long and we're here in bed. This is shameful behavior, Acton."

The sound of Stephanie's drowsy voice broke through the taunting warning winding its way through his head and he gazed down at the crown of her head tucked beneath his chin.

"It's shameful, all right," he agreed. "A shame that it took us so long to get here."

Laughing softly, she turned in his arms so that she was facing him and as Acton looked into her glistening blue eyes, he knew his heart had never felt so full or content.

"Do you know what I feel like at this very moment?" she asked.

"Hungry?"

Another chuckle shook her chest, "No. I feel like a princess with the world at her feet."

His smile came from the depths of his heart. "Well, you have kissed a frog."

"And he turned into a handsome prince." She stretched her neck upward until she could press her lips to his. "That kiss is to make sure you don't turn back into a frog."

Certain that the tender feelings swelling his chest were exposed on his face, he buried it in her silky hair and tried to not to sound like he was being strangled. "Thank you for saving me from that fate."

Her sigh fanned the side of his neck as she slipped an arm around his waist. "Seymour deserves a special treat and I'm going to give him one."

"For what? Being a furry little beast?"

She gave his back a gentle pinch. "Seymour is a sweetheart. If it hadn't been for him having that scratching spell I might not have ever met you."

Amused, he lifted his head and gave her an impish look. "Hmm. You're right. I might just give him a T-bone steak for introducing the two of us."

The playful twinkle in her eyes dimmed as she traced a fingertip over his cheek and down to the corner of her lips. "Then you don't regret us? This?"

Making love to Stephanie had upended everything about the man he'd ever thought he was or would be. And no matter what happened in the future, he knew this time in her arms would play a part in shaping his life.

"I've been wanting us to be together, Stephanie. And you've given me so much. So much." Threading his fingers into her hair, he pressed a line of kisses over her cheek and down the length of her straight little nose before he settled on her lips. "No regrets, my darling. This is only the beginning for us."

"Yes, our sweet beginning." She'd breathed the words against his lips, and now opened her mouth to receive his kiss, wrapped an arm around his neck and snuggled her soft body next to his.

Desire stirred deep within him and the reaction had Acton wondering what was happening to him. The sweat hadn't yet dried on his body and he was already wanting to be back inside her.

With intentions of deepening the embrace, he

rolled her onto her back, but that was as far as he got before Linus let out a whimper.

At the same time, they turned their heads in the direction of the baby. As if on cue, Linus let out a hungry howl that said he wasn't to be ignored.

"I need to get him," she said. "It's time for his bottle."

She started to rise, but he put a hand on her shoulder. "You stay put. I'll tend to Linus. Tonight you're my princess, remember? And your prince wants to pamper you."

Acton climbed off the bed and was reaching for his jeans, when from the corner of his eye, he spotted Stephanie sliding off the bed to join him.

As she plucked her sweater and jeans from the floor, he turned to her. "What are you doing? Don't you trust me to take care of Linus?"

Shaking back her tousled red hair, she stepped over and placed a hand on his arm. "We're together now. And that's how we're going to take care of Linus—together."

In spite of the baby's angry cries, Acton took a moment to lean over and press a quick kiss to her lips.

She was too good for him, he thought. And sooner or later, she would realize she could do much better than a simple cowboy. But he'd already planted his boots in both stirrups. He had no choice but to ride to the bitter end.

Chapter Twelve

Stephanie laughed as Mack and Tallulah chased after the tennis ball she'd thrown toward the end of the long fenced run. With Tallulah's short dachshund legs, she had to work twice as hard to keep up with the terrier, but neither of the small dogs could beat Buddy to the ball.

Proud of his accomplishment, the bigger dog trotted back to Stephanie and dropped the prize at her feet.

"Buddy, I think we can safely pronounce your leg fit as a fiddle. But if you want to keep Mack and Tallulah as your friends, you're going to have to lag back and let them win some of the time."

The dog whined and Stephanie was fondly petting the back of his neck, when she heard footsteps behind her.

Turning, she was more than surprised to see her three brothers standing near the entrance of the chain-link enclosure. *Now what were they up to?* she wondered as she saw Steven motion for her to join them.

Giving the three dogs final pats on the head, Stephanie walked down the run to where her brothers continued to wait.

"What's wrong?" she asked as she got within hearing distance. "Has something happened?"

Steven was the one to answer. "No. We'd like to talk with you. And since you've been gone so much lately, we wanted to catch you while you're home."

Home. Strange how the last two and half weeks had changed her feelings about that one special word. Although her brothers didn't know it, the Fame and Fortune Ranch didn't feel like home to her anymore. Her suite of rooms, which were so lavishly furnished and supplied with anything and everything she could possibly need, didn't feel nearly as comfortable and inviting as Acton's old farmhouse.

Steven opened the gate to let her out of the dog run, then shut it carefully behind her.

Callum said, "Let's go sit by the pool and get comfortable."

Stephanie didn't have time to get comfortable.

She'd promised Acton that she and Linus would be over at his house by seven this evening.

"I can't get too comfortable. I have a date," she said.

Dillon cleared his throat and the awkward glances exchanged among the three brothers didn't go unnoticed by Stephanie.

"Okay, what is this about? You three look like kids caught with your hands in the cookie jar."

Callum pointed to a cushioned chaise lounge. "Sit down, Stephanie. We won't keep you long. We promise."

To keep the peace, she took a seat. Steven sat down in a chair opposite her, while Callum and Dillon chose to remain standing.

"Is something going on with Mom and Dad? Or our sisters?" Normally, Stephanie tried to talk with the family back in Fort Lauderdale on a weekly basis, but she'd been so busy these past few days that she'd not taken the time to call or text.

"No. They're all fine," Dillon assured her.

"It's you that we're worried about," Steven said. "You've been going out practically every night for the past two weeks and—"

Seeing where the conversation was headed, Stephanie held up a hand. "That is my business. Just like where you three go is your business. I don't try to butt into your lives, so why are you trying to butt into mine? It's ridiculous!"

"Ridiculous? Really?" Steven said, shooting the questions back at her. "How many times have we seen you locked away in your room, crying your heart out because some jerk called it quits?"

Stephanie couldn't believe how much she wanted to reach over and slap her brother's face.

"Listen, Steven, maybe you think you're trying to protect me, but what you're doing to me is worse than dealing with a no-account boyfriend! I need for the three of you to believe in me! To trust me to use good judgment—not just about men, but every important decision. Instead, you treat me like a silly teenager with her head in the clouds."

From the smirk on Steven's face, she could see her remarks had rolled off his back without making a dent in his mind-set. "Have you ever stopped to think that's what you're acting like?" he asked.

Callum sighed, then said, "Look, Stephanie, you're a Fortune. That makes things different for you."

She looked at him with disbelief. "Are you saying that makes me better than other people? Better than Acton?"

Callum shook his head. "That's not what I'm implying at all. It just means that there are some people out there who might want to take advantage of us—of you—because you are a Fortune. We just want you to take things slowly before you jump into a situation where you might get hurt."

In spite of her being a foster mother to Linus and her new newfound feelings for Acton, her brothers couldn't see that she was changing and evolving into a much stronger woman. They still saw her as gullible Stephanie, who'd never been able to pick a worthwhile man for herself. The idea cut her deeply.

Swallowing at the ball of emotion in her throat, she said, "So you think Acton is out to use me. Or he's after my money. Is that it?"

"Stephanie! We didn't say anything like that!" Dillon scolded."

"No. You didn't have to," she said bitterly. "It's pretty obvious that you're all afraid I'm getting hooked up with a loser—again."

"Look, Stephanie," Stephen spoke up, "We're not judging Acton. We don't even know him—yet. We just want you to take your time and use your head. Not just your heart."

Acton had opened her eyes and her heart, Stephanie thought. But trying to convince her brothers of that would be useless.

"Look, you three, I appreciate the fact that you want me to be happy. If that's the real purpose behind this meeting," she added crossly.

"What is that supposed to mean?" Steven asked, "What other motive would we have, except your happiness?"

"I'm not sure. Maybe all this high-rolling and wheeling and dealing you three have been doing around Rambling Rose has gone to your heads. Maybe you're afraid I might marry my cowboy and that would embarrass all of you!"

"Oh, Stephanie!" Callum rolled his eyes. "It's not that at all!"

Steven actually jumped to his feet. "Are you planning on marrying this Donovan guy?"

Was she already dreaming about becoming Acton's wife? Of being the mother of his children? Even if she was, she had no idea if Acton's future plans were headed in the same direction as hers. Yes, she'd spent every available night she could find with him, and during that time, their passion for each other hadn't dimmed. It had only grown hotter. But that didn't mean he was in love with her. Or that he wanted to make her his wife.

Yet even with the uncertainty of her future looming before her, Stephanie had never been so happy and she wasn't about to let her three meddling brothers spoil it for her.

Jumping to her feet, she said, "I'd never tell you three what my personal plans are. You'd only try to ruin them!"

She hurried toward the house, leaving her brothers staring worriedly after her.

In spite of the drizzly morning, Acton, Shawn and their dad were trying to finish building a section of fence when the last spool of barbed wire they'd been stretching reached the end.

"Well, that's it for now," his father said as he tossed the empty spool into the back of his pickup truck. "It's almost time for lunch, anyway. After I eat, I'll drive into Rambling Rose and pick up a few more spools of wire. You guys go do what you want until I get back."

The tall, lean man was in his midfifties, but looked and worked like a man twenty years younger. As Acton watched him step up into the truck and drive across the open pasture, he wondered if his mother had brought up the subject of Acton seeing Stephanie to his father. So far his dad hadn't mentioned a word to him, but that didn't mean he was unaware of his son's new girlfriend. Ramsey Donovan had always been the kind of father who thought it best to let his older children make their own decisions—and their own mistakes—in order to learn from them.

"I think I'll go back to the ranch house and eat with Mom and Dad," Shawn said. "I didn't bring any lunch with me, did you?"

"No. I'm going to drive into Rambling Rose and see if Stephanie can get away from Paws and Claws long enough to have lunch," he told his brother.

The other man grinned. "So it's gotten to the point where seeing her at night isn't enough for you."

Acton darted him an annoyed look. "What would you know about it, anyway?"

"Ha! I'm not blind, Acton. Neither is the rest of the family. We've been seeing Stephanie's car parked at your place. You two have been keeping some pretty late hours."

Acton tugged his hat down lower on his forehead and hoped it shaded the red blush creeping over his face.

"She'd rather come to my house than me go to hers."

Shawn's eyebrows arched with speculation. "Why? Because those snobbish brothers of hers don't want you around?"

Acton grimaced. "They're not snobs, Shawn. Not really. They're just concerned about their sister's happiness."

"How can you be so benevolent? You told me they treated you like a doormat that night you were helping Stephanie with the baking. Have you talked with them since then?"

"No. But I plan to. Soon. They don't understand what they're doing to their sister." It had taken him hours to calm her down from her brothers' so-called "advice" when she'd finally arrived at his place last night.

Shawn shook his head. "By disapproving of you? Hell, Acton. I wouldn't be talking to those guys—I'd be landing a few blows on their jaws."

Acton rolled his eyes. "That would really show what a good guy I am."

Shawn put a hand on Acton's shoulder and pushed him toward the old work truck they'd driven to this isolated part of the ranch. "You know what they say about good guys, Acton. They always wind up with the short end of the stick. Think about it."

Acton did think about it throughout the drive to Rambling Rose and even while he was sitting across from Stephanie in the fast-food restaurant. Making love to her had changed him in ways he'd never expected. Shawn would probably say she was making him soft and wimpy, but that really wasn't the case. Loving her had given him the ability to see things through her eyes and it had made the world a different place for him.

Loving her. Had he already fallen in love with Stephanie? Was that what was causing the emptiness he felt whenever he was away from her? Oh, Lord, he might as well admit, at least to himself, just how smitten he was with the redheaded beauty.

"I'm glad you could get away for lunch," he told her as he watched her bite into a cheeseburger. "You know I was thinking that for the exception of the Valentine fund-raiser, you and I haven't been out on the town on a regular kind of date. How would you like to go to dinner one night? To a special place— just you and me?"

"Without Linus?"

She looked crushed, but Acton didn't let her response put him off. "You deserve to treat yourself once in a while, Stephanie. Even parents hire babysitters and go out on occasion."

With a nod of acquiescence, she said, "Yes, you're right, Acton. I just feel…guilty about it, because I'm away from him during the day while I'm at work. And I hate to ask Becky to watch him. She has her hands full with her twins and then she'd tell Callum why I needed a sitter and he—"

"Wouldn't like it," Acton said grimly, finishing her thought. "Well, I can't make Callum like me, but I can fix the babysitter issue. Mom would be only too happy to watch the little guy."

Her mouth fell open. "I haven't even met your mother! Gina is the only member of your family that I've met."

"That's something I want to change…soon."

Her blue eyes wandered over his face as though she couldn't believe what he was saying.

He reached across the table and took her hand. "Would you like to meet my parents?"

A smile curved the corners of her lips. "I would love to meet your family, Acton. I just hope they approve of me spending time with their son."

"They will," he promised. "Just wait and see."

The muffled ring of a phone suddenly sounded from her purse and she frowned at the interruption.

"Excuse me, Acton, I should look at this. It could be the clinic."

He nodded his understanding and she took the call. The conversation was short, with Stephanie uttering only a few words. By the time she ended the call, her face was paper-white, her eyes wide. To say she looked stunned would be an understatement.

"Stephanie, what's happened?"

She looked over at him and he could see tears pooling in her eyes.

"That was Dr. Green," she said in a strained voice. "He had some news for me."

Acton frowned. "I'm sorry. Who is Dr. Green?"

"He's the head pediatrician at Rambling Rose Pediatric Center. He's the doctor who came to Laurel's aid when she first went into labor at the ribbon-cutting ceremony."

"Laurel—you're talking about Linus's biological mother?"

Nodding, she thrust the phone back into her purse. "I'm sorry, Acton. I can't eat. Would you mind if we get out of here? I'll explain when we get outside."

"No problem. Let's go."

Acton hurriedly gathered up the remainder of their meal and tossed it into the trash receptacle on the way out the door. Once they reached his truck, he helped her into the passenger seat, then took his place behind the steering wheel.

"Do you need to go see this Dr. Green?" he asked. "Is this something about Linus?"

Her expression sick, she said, "I don't need to see Dr. Green. But it is about Linus. And I—I feel like my whole world has just turned upside down, Acton. I don't know any other way to say it. Dr. Green says that Linus's father has been located and he's coming to Rambling Rose. I've known from the very start that it was a possibility that he or the mother might show up, but I... A part of me wanted to think that it might not happen. That I could end up being Linus's adopted mother."

Acton could understand why she felt her world was upended. He felt like someone had just whammed him in the head with a two-by-four. "Linus's father? But with the mother saying he was out of the picture I assumed the guy probably didn't want the baby. Looks like my assumption was wrong." Shaking his head, he suddenly backtracked. "But maybe I'm wrong in thinking he does want the baby. Just because he's coming to Rambling Rose doesn't mean he wants to be a full-time parent to little Linus. It might just mean that he's willing to help locate the mother."

Stephanie shook her head. "He'd hardly need to come to Rambling Rose for that reason, Acton. No, it's obvious. He's coming for his son—my little baby—at least, my temporary baby!"

By the time the last words came out of her mouth, she was sobbing and Acton was sure his heart was going to break for her as he reached across the console and dragged her into his arms.

"Don't cry, Stephanie. Everything will work out. Right now, you are Linus's legal foster mother and this man might not even be able to prove he is the father."

Sniffing, she drew her head back from his shoulder and used the back of her hand to wipe her teary eyes. "You're right, Acton. I can't fall apart now. I need to wait and see what this man is planning."

"Did Dr. Green know when he'd be arriving in Rambling Rose?"

She shook her head. "He's going to call me back as soon as he gets all the details."

Acton could only wonder what this was going to do to him and Stephanie. He knew, probably more than anyone, just how much Stephanie considered Linus to be her own baby. If this mystery man took him away from her, he wasn't sure she could deal with the heartache. He knew one thing for sure—he wanted to be with her, to reassure her that no matter what happened with Linus, he'd be there to support her.

Later that afternoon, between patients, Stephanie informed Dr. Neil that she needed to take a few minutes off to speak with Dr. Green at the pediatric center. The veterinarian was more than obliging and told Stephanie there was no need for her to hurry. Dayna could assist him until she returned.

On the short drive over to the new pediatric building, Stephanie prayed that the doctor could give her more details about Linus's father. Mainly, what the man's intentions might be. But deep down, she had the sickening feeling that this was the beginning of the end of her tenure as the baby's mother.

Thankfully, Dr. Green's afternoon schedule wasn't too hectic for him to spare a few minutes to speak with Stephanie.

When a nurse ushered her into his office, the fatherly man with a head full of white hair and matching beard left his executive chair and greeted her with a gentle pat on her shoulder.

"Have a seat, Stephanie," he said, gesturing to a comfortable chair in front of his desk. "I'm glad you came. I realize my news had to be jarring."

She attempted to swallow away the ball of fear that had been stuck in her throat ever since she and Acton had left the fast-food restaurant.

"I won't lie, Dr. Green. It has shaken me. I mean, it's always been in the back of my mind that Laurel might return for her son and I'd have to give him over. And I knew there had to be a father somewhere who might want his child. But the more I grew to love Linus, the more I let myself push those possibilities to the back of my mind."

"I understand, Stephanie," the doctor said with

empathy. "In your heart you've become the baby's mother."

Stephanie nodded glumly, then looked at him in question. "What does this man want? And how do we know he's actually the biological father?"

Folding his hands together on the desktop, the doctor said, "I've not spoken to him directly, but I think it's safe to assume he wants the child. He lives in Houston and I've spoken with social services there. The agency has ordered a DNA test on the man's behalf. Apparently he has some sort of letter proving he had a close relationship with Laurel."

Stephanie's head was swimming with questions, along with crushing images of seeing her baby whisked away by a stranger. Her brain refused to believe such a thing might happen, but her heart was telling her to prepare for the worst.

"A DNA test," she repeated in a hollow voice. "This man must feel certain that he's Linus's father."

With his white beard and hair and warm disposition, some of the children around Rambling Rose believed Dr. Green was actually Santa Claus. Now, as Stephanie looked to him for answers, she thought how wonderful it would be if he truly was Santa and could make her fondest wishes come true.

"It does sound that way," he agreed. "From what the woman with social services told me, this man has just now learned that Laurel had the baby and that Linus is here in Rambling Rose. As you might guess, he's very anxious to get the DNA results. So this evening when you pick up Linus at day care I need you to take him to the lab here in the clinic. I've already sent orders for a nurse to take a swab from his mouth. If we put a rush on it, we should see the results in a few days. Okay?"

On the inside, Stephanie felt like she was breaking into a thousand pieces, while on the outside she was gripping her hands together in her lap to keep them from shaking.

"Uh—yes, I'll take Linus by the lab. And then I guess we wait," she said as much to herself as to the doctor.

Dr. Green didn't immediately reply, and Stephanie looked across the desk to see he was regarding her with sympathy. The idea that he was already seeing the writing on the wall made her sick to her stomach.

"It's understandable that you've grown fond of Linus," he said. "But if this man does turn out to be Linus's father, then I think your heart will tell you what's right for the child."

Drawing in a breath, Stephanie called upon every ounce of inner strength she possessed to hold on to her composure.

"Have you heard anything about Laurel? Did this man know where to locate her?"

"She hasn't been located. But I was told this man might be able to help find her. Which would be a good thing. Don't you agree?"

Stephanie nodded. No matter how much she loved Linus, deep in her heart, she agreed that he deserved to have a real mother and father.

Rising to her feet, she said, "Thank you, Dr. Green, for taking the time to speak with me. I won't keep you any longer."

He joined her in front of the desk. "Anytime, Stephanie. I realize this whole situation is very unusual. As long as I've been a pediatrician I can't remember anything like this happening with a newborn. Especially here in Rambling Rose."

Bending her head, she fought against the tears glazing her eyes. "I'll be honest, Dr. Green, I was hoping to adopt Linus as my own. Now that—" She paused and drew in a shaky breath. "Well, it looks like that hope is over."

He took hold of her hand and gently patted the back of it. "Stephanie, you've been a very generous and loving foster mother for Linus. You should be proud of that. And you're still a very young woman. You'll have the opportunity to have babies of your own."

Yes, maybe, she thought. But Linus was already here. In her home, her arms, her life. She loved him. She didn't want to lose him.

Sniffing back her tears, she thanked the doctor again, then left his office before she broke down completely.

Thankfully, she managed to leave the pediatric

center without running into Becky. One look at her sister-in-law and she would have burst into a mess of hot tears.

When she returned to Paws and Claws, the waiting room was full of patients and the whole staff was too busy to ask her questions about leaving work in the middle of the afternoon.

Stephanie did her best to focus on her job, but Linus never left her mind for even a second, and by the time the clinic closed up for the evening, she was utterly exhausted.

As she left the building, she was thinking about her brothers and wondering how they were going to take the news about Linus, when she noticed Acton's truck was parked next to her vehicle.

Normally, the idea that he was waiting to see her would've sent her heart soaring with joy. This evening, she could hardly summon a smile.

"You look exhausted," he said as he met her on the sidewalk a few feet away from her parked car. "Has anything else happened about Linus?"

She let out a weary breath and he took her by the arm. "Let's go sit in your car. You can tell me there."

After they were comfortably seated in her little sedan, she said, "I went to see Dr. Green this afternoon. He informed me that I have to take Linus to the lab for a DNA swab."

"DNA! When?" Acton asked.

"This evening, when I pick him up from day care.

It seems this man from Houston believes he's Linus's father and he wants a test done as quickly as possible."

"Oh, God, that's not good."

Her eyes narrowed with speculation as she studied his face. "Not good? What does that mean? You've said before that Linus deserves a biological parent. And if you were Linus, wouldn't you be happy to know that at least one of your actual parents wanted you?"

He looked totally confused by her response. "Well, hell. Of course I would. But Linus is a baby. He doesn't know about that sort of thing right now. He only knows when someone holds him and loves him and feeds him. That someone is you."

"And you," she replied.

"That's right. And I'll just say it plainly—I don't want the little guy to be taken away. Real dad or no real dad. I realize that's probably selfish of me, but I can't help it."

By the time he'd finished, Stephanie was crying and she didn't bother to try to hide her tears. She was too tired, too afraid to do anything about stemming her overwrought emotions.

"You're not making me feel any better about this, Acton."

His expression turned to one of disbelief. "What does that mean? I don't want you to lose Linus any more than you do!"

"I know. But we need to be reasonable about this situation. Linus isn't my baby. Nor is he yours."

"Well, it sure as hell feels like he's yours—ours. And where was this guy when Linus was born? Why wasn't he with the woman he supposedly loved enough to make a child with?"

Stephanie had been asking herself the same questions. But the answers weren't going to change the facts. "There could be good reasons he wasn't around when Linus was born. Laurel might not have told him she was pregnant. She might have disappeared from his life before he had any idea she was going to have his child. Without any facts, we can't blame him for not being around when Linus was born."

He let out a heavy breath. "Nothing about this situation feels right, Stephanie."

"Whether it feels right or not, it's happening."

He reached over and gently touched the wet trail of tears on her face. "I'm sorry, Stephanie. I realize I'm not handling this very well. And that's making things worse for you."

She looked at him. "I understand how attached you've become to Linus."

Pain shadowed his eyes and though Stephanie wanted to him help him feel better, she couldn't. She was too crushed with her own pain to hardly know what she was saying.

He nodded. "Deep down...well, I know it would

be best for Linus to have his real dad. And probably best for you. It's just that right now it hurts to think of losing him."

She shook her head. "Yes, it hurts. But we no longer have a choice in the matter. Anyway, I need to go pick up Linus from day care and get the swab done before I head home."

Frowning with confusion, he asked, "Home? Aren't you coming to my house tonight? That's what we'd planned, remember?"

She looked at him blankly. Everything was barreling at her from all directions, tearing at her thoughts and emotions. She had to have space to collect herself. To think. "Yes, I remember. But things have changed since then. I need to speak with my brothers about Linus—"

His brows arched upward. "Your brothers? I'm the guy who's been Linus's stand-in dad. Doesn't that count for something?"

She blew out a frustrated breath. "Of course it does. But my brothers—"

"Yes, I see. You feel it's important that you be with them now," he interrupted, his voice stiff. "So go."

"You don't have to be so cold about it," she retorted.

"I'm not being cold. I'm being realistic. It's obvious you believe your brothers can help you with baby Linus much more than I can. And you're probably right. They have the clout and the means. All I have is my heart. And—well, none of that matters. I can see that now."

She glared at him. "That's not what I'm thinking! And I don't deserve this from you, Acton! Especially now!"

"You're right, Stephanie. You don't deserve it." His jaw tight, he opened the door and climbed out of the car.

"Where are you going?" she asked, stunned that he was leaving like this.

"You can handle this situation far better without me," he said flatly. "In fact, I figure your whole life will be better without me in it."

With that he slammed the door and went straight to his truck.

Numb with pain, Stephanie waited until he'd driven away before she started the car and left the parking lot.

As she drove to the pediatric center, she couldn't decide which was worse—the reality that everything she'd ever had with Acton had just ended, or that this might be the last time she'd be collecting her baby from day care.

Chapter Thirteen

Four days later, Stephanie stood in the bathroom and stared in shock at the result of the home-pregnancy test.

Positive.

It shouldn't be surprising. Her period was several days late and the mere thought of breakfast was enough to make her stomach feel like she was on a bobbing sailboat. Still, she was amazed that she'd gotten pregnant. She'd been taking her pills regularly and had never missed a one.

The only birth control that's foolproof is abstinence. The advice of her ob-gyn back in Fort Lauderdale had mostly drifted through one ear and out the other. Even when the doctor had been writing Stephanie's prescription, she'd warned her that having sex while on the Pill could produce a pregnancy. At that time, Stephanie's last boyfriend had ended their relationship because she'd refused to give him an interest-free loan to buy a fishing boat. Sex had been the last thing on her mind. All she'd wanted was something strong enough to keep her periods from popping up way too early. She'd had no way of knowing then that she'd eventually be falling into bed with a virile cowboy.

Now she was going to have Acton's baby. Oh, Lord, how ironic!

Overwhelmed, she placed a protective hand over the region of her womb and leaned heavily against the vanity. She'd not spoken to Acton since that evening they'd argued in the Paws and Claws parking lot. What was he going to think about this development? Being a daddy to Linus for a few hours at a time wasn't the same as being a full-time parent. Was he prepared for that much commitment?

Deep down, she believed Acton was a good man with good intentions. But he was only twenty-five and anyone who knew him said he was far from ready to settle down with a wife and children.

So why did you fall into bed with him, Stephanie? Why did you leap into his arms and let yourself dream about a future with him?

Because she loved him. Truly loved him, she answered the chastising voice in her head. But what good was love going to do her now? Acton thought she didn't need him. That she didn't want to include him in the important aspects of her life. How was she going to make him see that he was wrong?

A wave of nausea washed over her and she leaned over the sink and splashed cold water on her face in an effort to ease her heaving stomach.

It didn't matter how Acton reacted to the news that he was going to be a father, she firmly told herself. For years she'd wanted a baby and dreamed about being a mother. Now that she was actually pregnant, even under such dismal circumstances, she was happy that they'd created a child together.

Acton removed the saddle from the bay horse tied at the hitching post and carried it into the tack room. Right behind him, Shawn carried an armload of saddle blankets and bridles.

The two brothers had spent most of the morning riding the back pastures, checking on late calving cows. It was a job that Acton normally loved. Anytime he could spend a few hours on a horse, he was in heaven. But today he'd simply gone through the motions. But then, ever since he and Stephanie had parted ways, he'd been living on automatic pilot.

"I'm glad Dad is driving over to San Antonio this afternoon to see about buying that hay baler he's had his eye on," Shawn said. "If we work like hell while he's gone, we can finish the fence and surprise him."

With a mocking grunt, Acton lifted the saddle onto a wooden stand and jerked the fenders into place. "He'd be surprised, all right. He thinks we can't do anything right without him watching over our shoulders."

Frowning, Shawn hung the wet blankets on a hook to allow them to dry. "That's not true and you know it. What the hell is wrong with you, anyway? You haven't said more than a dozen words this morning and most of them have been sarcastic."

Closing his eyes, Acton lifted his hat from his head and combed fingers through is hair. "Sorry, Shawn," he said ruefully. "I hadn't realized I was being so surly. I've been—"

"A real jerk," Shawn interrupted as he walked over to where Acton stood. "What's up?"

Acton's nostrils flared as he sucked in a weary breath. "Nothing. I'm just not feeling well, that's all."

Unconvinced, Shawn shook his head. "Try again. You're not sick. You're miserable about something. And I have a feeling it's that Fortune woman. Acton, I tried to tell you—"

"Damn it, Shawn, I don't need to be preached at by you! Things are bad enough as it is and—"

Shawn interrupted. "What things? What's happened?"

Shaking his head with defeat, Acton sat down on

an upended feed bucket and quickly explained about Linus and how a man claiming to be his father has requested a DNA test.

"You think this man is legitimate?" Shawn asked.

Acton shrugged. "He must have good reason to believe he's the father. But I can't say for sure. Stephanie and I haven't spoken since the day she got the news. She'd rather be with her brothers. They're more capable of helping her deal with a crisis than me, apparently," he said sarcastically. "And you're right, Shawn, I should've listened to you and Mom. Stephanie will never see me as an equal. Or as a man who can take care of her."

"Aren't you being a little hard on yourself, Acton? And on her?"

"I'm just trying to be real, Shawn. And right now reality hurts like hell." He wiped a hand over his face, then stared blindly at the toes of his boots. "I'll admit that when we got the news about Linus I didn't handle things too well. But to be honest, Shawn, I was just as cut up as she was over the whole idea that someone might be going to be taking our baby away."

"Our baby?"

He didn't try to hide the pain in his eyes as he looked up at his brother. "I guess that sounds foolish to you. But Linus was beginning to feel like my son, too. Now he's—" Acton swallowed. "Well, it looks like there's a strong possibility he'll be going to go live with his real dad. And there's not a damned thing I can do to stop it."

"So the both of you were scared and hurting and you lashed out at each other. That's understandable. Have you thought about reaching out to her, trying to apologize? I'm not saying she's right and you're wrong, Acton, I'm just saying one of you has to extend an olive branch."

"I don't think she'll accept an olive branch or anything else from me," Acton said dully.

Shawn opened his mouth to reply at the same time Acton's phone dinged with an incoming text message.

"I'd better check this. It might be Dad." He pulled the phone from his pocket and was immediately shocked to see a message from Dillon Fortune. "What the hell?"

"What is it? Has Dad blown a tire or something?"

Acton gripped the phone as he tapped the screen to open the message. "No. It's from Stephanie's brother, Dillon." After rapidly scanning the short text, he said in a stunned voice, "He and his brothers are worried about her. They'd like for me to come speak with them."

"Seriously?"

Dazed, Acton rose from his seat on the bucket. "Yes. He says if I can get away, they'll be at their office in the work yard across from the Shoppes."

"Are you going?"

Groaning, Acton lifted his gaze to the dusty cobwebs hanging from the rafters of the tack room. "Yes. But I don't get any of this. They don't approve of me. At least, that's the feeling I get from them. So what could they want?"

"To hell with them!" Shawn boomed. "They need to know you don't approve of them!"

Shaking his head, Acton began unbuckling his chaps. "No, Shawn. This is not about me and them. Not now. It's about Stephanie and what's best for her. No matter what, I want her to be happy. Even if that means I have to step out of her life—permanently."

Shawn's eyes narrowed shrewdly and then his mouth fell open. "You really love this woman, don't you?"

Acton had been asking himself that very question for the past several days. Funny how it had taken a simple text from her brother to allow him to see the answer plain and clear.

"Yes. I do love her. Somehow I have to make her understand that."

Shawn gave his shoulder an affectionate squeeze. "You go show the Fortunes they're not dealing with a hayseed."

Even though horse manure was probably dried around the edges of his boots and dust had turned his black hat to brown, Acton didn't waste time changing into clean clothes. He drove straight to The Shop-

pes, where several pickup trucks and other work vehicles were parked around the modular building that
served as the makeshift office of Fortune Brothers
Construction.

Off to one side, three workers were loading scaf-
folds onto the back of a long, flatbed trailer, while a
few feet away, a heating-and-cooling van braked to
a halt. Dust billowed from the wheels as the driver
jumped out and hurried into the office.

Acton followed at a slower pace, and after placing
a brief knock on the door, he stepped inside a long
room furnished with a desk at each end and a group-
ing of comfortable furniture in between.

All three of Stephanie's brothers were present,
along with the man who'd jumped out of the van. All
turned to look at Acton and then the man behind one
of the desks the one he remembered as Steven, rose
and walked over to greet him.

"Hello, Mr. Donovan. We're glad you could
come."

He reached out to shake hands and Acton politely
complied. "Hello, Mr. Fortune."

He inclined his head toward the two men walking
over to join them. "I imagine you remember Dillon
and Callum."

Dillon was dressed in jeans, boots and a plaid
Western shirt. He looked much like the natives of
Rambling Rose, while Callum and Steven were both
in khakis and ties and appeared as though they'd

be more comfortable in a high-rise office in downtown Houston.

Acton shook hands with the other two men and Steven gestured toward the couch and armchairs. "Let's sit."

While the four men took their seats, the van guy grabbed a handful of papers from one of the desks and discreetly let himself out of the office.

"I'm sure you're wondering what this is about," Callum said.

Acton tried not to grimace. "You three haven't exactly invited me to be friends. So, yeah, I'm wondering."

To Acton's surprise, Dillon appeared regretful. "I can't speak for my brothers, but I'm sorry about that, Acton. It's not that we had anything against you personally. It's more like we, uh, we worry about Stephanie. She's been hurt too many times."

"So why worry now? Stephanie has ended things with me. She's apparently seen things your way."

Steven was stunned. "We didn't tell her to end things with you! In fact, she hasn't mentioned anything about the two of you. When did this happen?"

So, Acton thought sickly, he wasn't important enough to Stephanie for her to mention him, even as an afterthought.

Acton said, "The day the doctor ordered her to take Linus in for a DNA swab."

Callum nodded with sudden dawning. "I'm beginning to see. She was very distraught that night. We thought it was all about Linus."

"She was heartbroken," Acton said in a clipped tone. "Over Linus, not me. So now you don't need to worry about Stephanie any longer. She's free to date anyone she wants."

The brothers exchanged troubled glances before Steven leveled a pointed look at Acton. "Is that what you want? To step out of Stephanie's life?"

"Hell no!" he retorted, then cleared his throat and said, "I mean, I want Stephanie to be happy. That's what's important to me. I, uh, well… I wish that she still cared about me. Because my feelings for her are very serious. Maybe she didn't understand that. Or maybe she did understand and it didn't matter to her. I was seeing me and her and Linus as a family. But now that Linus might be going away, I guess everything is over."

The brothers kept looking at each other as if they were totally confused.

It was Steven who finally said, "We've made a mistake about you, Acton. We thought you were probably just playing Stephanie along. She's beautiful and rich and unfortunately a bit gullible."

"So you three think," Acton said, his voice brittle. "I happen to think she's very smart and special. And her heart is bigger than her head."

"Look," Callum said, "we don't know what was said between you two, but we do know that Stephanie is in a bad way. And we believe you might be able to help."

"How? Before I left to come over here, I tried texting her. So far she's ignored my message. I figure she'll keep on ignoring me."

Dillon said, "Eric Johnson, Linus's father, and a social worker will be coming to the ranch this evening to collect Linus. We don't have to tell you that once the baby is gone, Stephanie is going to be crushed."

Acton felt as if he'd been punched. "You mean the test results are back? The man actually is Linus's father?"

Callum nodded. "The test has determined that Eric is the father."

Acton mulled over the jarring news. Stephanie's heart must be tearing right down the middle, he thought sickly.

Steven cast him a hopeful glance. "We thought you might try to see Steph tomorrow. After she's had tonight to pull herself together."

Acton scooted to the edge of the chair. "What makes you think she'd want to see me tomorrow? Or even agree to see me?"

Callum was the one to answer. "Before this matter with Linus's father came up, Stephanie was happier than we'd ever seen her. We all agree that part of that happiness had to do with you. If you say you're serious about our sister, then we ask that you don't give up on her. She needs you now...more than ever."

This was the last thing Acton had expected to hear from Stephanie's brothers, and though it made him feel somewhat better, he still had a multitude of doubts.

"I'm not sure how forgiving Stephanie might be," Acton said. "But I promise you, I'm not giving up."

At Paws and Claws, Stephanie was in the recovery room, checking on recuperating patients, when Dayna stuck her head in the door.

"Do you have time for one more patient?" she asked.

"Dr. Neil left the building about five minutes ago," Stephanie answered.

"I know. He stopped by the front desk on his way out. But you're still here. And a woman has come in with her cat. She says he's limping on his front paw."

Stephanie glanced at her watch as she walked over to where Dayna stood. "It's still a half hour before we close the doors. I suppose I could have a look."

"That's what I thought you'd say." Dayna shot her a coy grin, then turned to leave. "I'll put them in Exam Room 3."

Sensing Dayna was holding something back, Stephanie called out. "Wait, Dayna! Just who is this woman?"

Her smile even wider, Dayna glanced over her shoulder at Stephanie. "Faye Donovan."

Acton's mother? Wait—could he have sent her on his behalf? No! That was a ridiculous thought. Acton would never let anyone do his talking for him. Even so, how was she going to face Faye Donovan? This child she was carrying was going to be the woman's grandchild. What would she think if she knew?

Dayna suddenly stepped closer. "You look pale, Stephanie. Are you okay? I can tell Mrs. Donovan to come back tomorrow."

Putting the meeting off wouldn't help Stephanie. It would only cause the cat to suffer longer than need be.

Squaring her shoulders, she said, "Don't do that. I'm okay—just a bit tired. We've had a very busy day."

Dayna blew out a weary breath as she turned to leave. "You telling me. I'm going to be seeing cats and dogs in my sleep."

With Dayna gone, Stephanie smoothed a hand over her hair, then straightened the white lab coat she was wearing over her moss green blouse. This wasn't the way she'd envisioned meeting Acton's mother, but now that he'd apparently walked out of Stephanie's life, she supposed it hardly mattered where she met the woman.

Down the long hallway, Stephanie rapped her knuckles on the door of Exam Room 3, then stepped inside. Standing next to the examination table was a tall, slim woman with short blond hair. Somewhere in her fifties, she had soft, pretty features that faintly resembled Acton's sister, Gina. She was dressed casually in jeans, cowboy boots and a denim jacket. But it was the gentle smile on her face that caught Stephanie's attention.

"Hello. I'm Stephanie Fortune," she introduced herself.

The woman offered her hand. "I'm Faye Donovan."

Stephanie shook her hand, while hoping she didn't look as nervous as she felt. "It's nice to meet you."

"Please, just call me Faye. All my friends do."

Was she implying she wanted them to be friends? Oh Lord, just how much did Faye know about her son's relationship with Stephanie? Didn't she know it was over between them? Except that it couldn't ever be over entirely, Stephanie thought sickly. Not with the baby coming.

Clearing her throat, she said, "All right. And please, call me Stephanie."

"Thanks, I will." Smiling again, Faye gestured to the cat carrier. "Samson seems to have something wrong with his paw. I tried to look at it myself, but he's not the most cooperative cat on the ranch."

"Dr. Neil has already left for the day," Stephanie explained. "But I'll see what I can do for him. If that's okay."

"That would be great," Faye said brightly. "Samson is an outdoor cat and he loves to roam and get into mischief. I'm thinking he might have stepped on a mesquite thorn."

"That's possible," Stephanie agreed, while Faye unlatched the door on the carrier. "Is he friendly with strangers?"

"The only thing I've ever seen Samson bite is another cat," Faye answered. "I can't predict how he'll react to you. But Acton says you're a genius with animals, so I'm sure you won't have a problem."

Yes, Acton had praised her work as a veterinarian assistant. But as a woman, she wasn't sure what he was thinking or feeling.

"I hope you're right," Stephanie replied.

Thankfully, it didn't take long for the large, black tomcat to cozy up to Stephanie and she quickly went about examining all four feet.

"Are you sure Samson was limping earlier?" Stephanie asked a few minutes later as she stroked the cat's back. "He appears to be walking up and down the exam table just fine and I don't find a thing wrong with any of his pads."

Stephanie didn't miss the sheepish expression stealing across Faye's face.

"Samson always was a little faker," she said. "He'll do anything for attention."

"I guess he's decided he's over his lameness now," Stephanie replied.

Faye's chuckle was riddled with guilt. "I'm sorry, Stephanie. You've caught me red handed. There's nothing wrong with Samson. I just used him as an excuse to see you."

Stephanie had already come to that conclusion. Still it was a surprise to hear Faye admit it.

"To see me? Why?"

Shaking her head, Faye said, "In spite of how this looks, I'm actually not an interfering mother. But this one time, it's just that I can see—the whole family can see—that Acton is in a bad way. He's not behaving like himself, at all. And I thought you might want to know. To talk with him. Maybe?"

These past few days since she and Acton had quarreled had been some of the worst of Stephanie's life. To think that Acton might be hurting, too, jarred her already ragged senses. "So he told you we argued?"

"No. The last time Acton mentioned you was when he asked me about having you over for dinner one night soon. I happily agreed. And then a day or two later, his mood just completely changed. He became a complete grouch, with hardly a word for anyone. His father and I didn't have to wonder what was wrong. We knew something must have gone wrong between the two of you."

The pain in Stephanie's chest was smothering her and she had to look away from Faye's perceptive gaze before she could speak. "I haven't heard from

Acton in the past few days. I think he's decided I'm not right for him."

Faye sighed. "And what about what you've decided? Do you feel the same way? That he's not right for you?"

The question caused Stephanie's gaze to swing back to Faye's concerned face. "No! I mean, I thought we were perfect for each other. And then…this thing with Linus's father happened and, well, now everything is just…awful."

Faye stepped forward and gently patted Stephanie's arm. "I'm sorry, Stephanie. God knows I didn't come here to upset you. I understand you have enough problems without my interference."

She had problems, all right, Stephanie thought glumly. Far more than Faye could know. "Then you know about Linus?"

Faye nodded. "Acton has talked a lot about you and the baby. When he told us about the father coming we could see he was crushed about the whole thing."

"Yes. So am I."

A moment of awkward silence passed and then Faye said, "I understand that you're probably thinking Acton isn't ready to settle down. It's no secret that he's dated plenty of women. I'm sure you've been told that. But until he met you he was never serious about any of them. Whatever you're thinking, Stephanie, he's a good, hard-working man. And he loves children. That's all I'm going to say. Except that I hope you two can patch things up, because I have a feeling you and I could be great friends."

With tears stinging the back of her eyes, Stephanie did her best to smile. "Thank you, Faye. I won't forget what you've said."

But in the end would it make any difference? Stephanie didn't know. The only thing she knew for certain was that Acton had chosen to walk away from her, and in the next few hours Linus would be out of her life. Those two realities were almost more than she could bear.

That evening, Stephanie and Linus, along with her three brothers, were in the great room of the Fame and Fortune Ranch house, waiting for Eric Johnson to arrive.

In the past days since Stephanie had spoken with child services and set up the meeting with Linus's father, Steven had taken it upon himself to research the man's background. He was thirty-five, a native of the Houston area and a wealthy businessman who owned a trucking firm that operated nationwide. He was currently single and from what information Steven had gathered, he'd been dating Linus's mother. But something had obviously gone awry between the two of them and Laurel had ended things abruptly.

Two days ago, Stephanie had spoken over the phone to the social worker dealing with Linus's case and the woman had explained that Eric had provided the agency with a letter that Laurel had written to him. He'd also produced signed documents from friends who knew both Laurel and Eric, stating that the two had been in a real relationship. The information had been enough to warrant a DNA test. And now he was coming to collect his son. His baby.

Each time those words tried to enter Stephanie's brain, she fought them like a tigress protecting her cubs. No matter what kind of papers Eric had provided, or what the lab test said, as far as she was concerned, Linus had been her baby for more than two months now. Everything inside her screamed that he belonged with her.

"Stephanie, are you okay? Would you like for me to put Linus in his bassinet?"

She looked around to see that Steven had come to stand next to the rocker, where she clung to Linus and hummed the Texas sandman lullaby to him.

Oh, God, if she could only turn back to all those times she and Acton and Linus had been together as a family. Her heart had been full then. Now it was nothing but a ragged ball of pain.

Acton is in a bad way. He's not behaving like himself at all. Faye's words drifted through her mind, causing the pain in her heart to intensify.

"No," she said hoarsely. "I want to hold him. This might be the last time."

He was studying her with a worried look when the doorbell suddenly rang. Stephanie flinched.

"I'll answer it," Callum offered.

When he returned to the great room, he was followed by a tall young man with light brown hair and a middle-aged woman wearing a plain dark suit.

Dillon and Steven promptly walked over to join them, while Stephanie remained frozen in the rocker, her fingers clenched to Linus's blanket.

She could hear her brothers introducing themselves, and then a few more pleasantries were exchanged before the man stepped away from the group and began walking toward her.

He was dressed in an expensive-looking sports jacket, dark slacks and a pair of Italian loafers. By the casual way he wore the clothing, Stephanie could tell he was a man who was accustomed to having the best of things.

He came to a stop a few feet in front of her chair and the knots that were already tying her stomach twisted even tighter. "You must be Stephanie," he said. "I'm Eric Johnson. Nice to meet you."

With Linus in her arms, she rose from the rocker and extended a hand to him. "Yes, I'm Stephanie," she said automatically. "It's nice to meet you, Mr. Johnson."

His gaze immediately dropped to Linus and a bright smile spread across his face. "So this is my son. I've been waiting for this moment and now that it's here, I, uh, well, I'm blown away. He's incredible!"

Her throat was clamped so tight she had to swallow twice before she could utter a reply. "Linus is a very special little guy."

His gaze was full of awe as he continued to look down at Linus. "Dr. Green has shared all his medical history, but you're the person who can tell me about his personality. Does he cry much?"

Since she'd learned of Eric Johnson's existence, she'd thought of him only as a shadowy figure who'd be taking Linus away from her. She'd not pictured him as a father seeing his baby for the first time. She'd not imagined him wanting this baby as much as she wanted him. She could see now how misguided her thinking had been.

Drawing in a bracing breath, she said, "Linus is a very good baby. If he cries it's usually because he's hungry or wants his diaper changed. He never has a tummy ache and only spits up on occasion. He loves his bottle and usually wakes just once in the night around two."

Eric extended his arms toward the baby. "If you don't mind, I'd really like to hold him."

"Of course." Her response sounded brittle, but he was too busy plucking Linus from her arms to notice.

Feeling as though she was about to crack into a million pieces, Stephanie watched him carefully position Linus in the crook of his arm.

"My son," he said with a wealth of tenderness. "You and I have lots of catching up to do."

I guess it would be best for Linus to have his real dad. And probably best for you.

As she watched a look of awe come over Eric Johnson's face, Acton's words drifted through her mind, haunting her with the truth. Even in Stephanie's distraught state of mind she could see this moment was monumental for him, and despite the pain she was feeling, she realized she couldn't resent the man for wanting his own child.

"Excuse me," she told him. "I need to speak with my brothers."

Leaving father and son, she walked across the room to her brothers and the social worker. The woman's features were haggard, her shoulders slumped. No doubt, the consequences of a stressful job, Stephanie concluded.

"I'm Margaret Malloy," she said, politely introducing herself to Stephanie. "I want to thank you, especially, for making this transfer easy for everyone concerned."

Easy? There wasn't anything easy about having her heart ripped out of her chest, Stephanie thought. But there was no point in piling her misery on this woman. It wasn't Margaret Malloy's fault that this series of events had touched all their lives.

"I want what's best for Linus," she said simply.

Sensing Stephanie's frazzled emotions, the agent

gave her an empathetic smile. "I'll go take a look at the baby and give you a few minutes alone with your brothers."

After the woman excused herself and walked away, Steven took one look at Stephanie's face and wrapped an arm around her shoulders. "Stay strong, honey. You'll get through this."

"Sure," she said stiffly. "I'll get through."

"You should take comfort in the fact that Eric appears to be a good guy," Callum said to her. "And he truly wants his son."

"What about Laurel?" Stephanie asked. "Has he heard from her?"

"No. But he has a few ideas about where she might've gone," Steven said. "He's already talked to the authorities about her."

"Hell of a way for a man to find out he's a father," Dillon said, lowering his voice so that only the four of them could hear. "Getting a letter from his ex-girlfriend telling him she was carrying his baby."

Steven said, "Yeah, that was bad enough. But he had no idea where she or his unborn child had gone to. It wasn't until he saw a news article about a woman going into labor in Rambling Rose, then later leaving the baby at the pediatric center and disappearing into the wild blue. He considered it a long shot that the story might be about Laurel, but he decided to look into it. I'm not sure how I'd handle that kind of shock to the senses."

Stephanie's eyes burned with unshed tears. "It's pretty obvious he's not going to change his mind and decide to leave Linus here with me."

Callum shook his head. "Sorry, honey. No chance of that happening. He's walking on air."

Drawing in a shuddering breath, she said, "I have Linus's things all packed. I'll go get them."

"I'll help you," Steven told her.

As soon as they returned from Stephanie's suite with Linus's belongings, Eric and the agent were ready to leave.

Thankfully, he was thoughtful enough to allow Stephanie a moment alone with Linus and she carried the baby to a private spot in the room.

"My sweet little boy, I love you so," she whispered as she smoothed a finger over his soft hair. "I have to tell you goodbye now. If Acton was here he'd tell you goodbye, too."

As though he understood, the baby let out a short cry and boxed the air with his little fist.

Smiling through her tears, she bent and placed a kiss on his forehead and drew in his baby scent one last time. Then, squaring her shoulders, she carried him back to his waiting father.

"Please keep me updated on how he's doing," she told him through the tightness in her throat.

"I will," he promised. "And thanks again for taking such good care of my son."

Seeing Stephanie was about to break apart, Callum quickly ushered the three toward the foyer. "I'll see you out," he told them.

Stephanie watched until Linus and his father disappeared. By then, Steven was at her side, patting her hand in an effort to console her.

"Linus has his father in his life now," he said. "Just concentrate on that good thought."

A real parent. In a little more than eight months she and Acton were going to be real parents. They just weren't going to be parents together.

Dillon stepped forward and peered closely at her face. "Stephanie? Are you okay? You look white."

As she looked helplessly at both brothers, her stomach roiled in protest.

"I—I'm sorry! I'm going to be sick!"

She raced to the nearest bathroom and as she threw up over the commode, she thought about Acton and how she was going to face him with the news about their baby.

Chapter Fourteen

Linus is now in Houston with his father. Get it together. Stephanie needs you.

Acton had been trying to force a few bites of breakfast down his throat this morning, when the text message from Dillon had arrived. And he'd had to read it several times over before the reality of it had finally sunk into his weary brain.

Linus was truly gone and he couldn't begin to imagine the pain that Stephanie must be going through. He wanted to console her. To take away all the hurt she was feeling. But did she really need him now? Would she forgive him for walking away? For not understanding?

These past few days without her, he'd been trying to convince himself that she was better off without him. That she'd be better off with a man who could give her all the things she was accustomed to having in her life. Things that he could never give her.

But now as he drove through the rain toward the Fame and Fortune Ranch, he desperately wanted to believe that his love would be enough for her.

After a fitful night, with hardly any sleep, Stephanie was in such an awful state, she was forced to call Paws and Claws and tell them she was too sick to make it into work. It was the first time she'd ever missed work for any reason and she felt guilty about it. But her brothers had convinced her she was right. She couldn't face work after going through the trauma of losing Linus.

What were her brothers going to think when they learned that not all of her misery was over Linus? That she was pregnant by the cowboy they'd feared would break her heart?

Oh, God, could it get any worse?

Finding no answers in the spring rain collecting in puddles on the walkway, she turned away from the window of her private suite in the ranch house and sat down on the couch.

After switching on a large, flat-screen TV attached to the opposite wall, she punched through dozens of channels before pushing the off button. She couldn't focus on anything. Her thoughts continued to vacillate between Linus and Acton.

Was the baby okay? Was Eric Johnson holding him, loving him? Was he doing all the things that Linus needed to be happy and healthy?

Her heart felt heavy, and she heaved out a sigh as she tried to accept the fact that she couldn't do anything about Linus now. But it was a different matter with Acton. Somehow she was going to have to find the strength to face him and tell him about the coming baby. Whether he had any deep feelings for her or not, he had a right to know that the two of them had created a child.

Eventually her pets must have sensed she needed comforting. Violet, the Siamese, curled up by her side, while, Daisy, the yellow tabby, settled herself in Stephanie's lap. Even Orville hopped over and snuggled his furry body next to her bare feet.

"Well, guys, at least you three love me. But it's going to be awfully quiet around here without Linus and Acton."

Violet let out a coarse meow and then another. Stephanie was stroking the cat and trying to blink away another stream of tears, when the doorbell rang.

The unexpected sound jolted her. Who could that be? Her brothers had left for the construction site earlier this morning and Becky and the twins were on their way to the pediatric center.

Easing away from the pets, Stephanie went to the front door and peeked out the peephole.

Acton!

Rain was dripping off the brim of his brown hat and the shoulders of his khaki Western shirt were splotched with wet spots. What was he doing here?

Her heart thumping fast, she opened the door and discovered her tongue had momentarily become glued to the roof of her mouth.

"Acton. What…why are you here?" she finally asked.

He gestured to the folded quilt and a plastic container jammed beneath one arm. "Your brothers told me you weren't feeling well. I thought you might need a little TLC. This is my grandmother's chicken soup and a favorite quilt of mine. It has dogs and cats on it, so I thought it might cheer you."

None of what he was saying sounded like a man who wanted to end things, Stephanie thought. And when she looked into his eyes, she was mystified to see there was no anger or accusation flashing back at her. What did any of this mean?

Totally confused, she asked, "My brothers? You've talked to them?"

His smile took on a wry slant. "I have."

She gestured for him to come in, and after he'd walked to the middle of the room, she shut the door and leaned her back against it.

"So you know that Linus is gone?" Even as she

asked the question, fresh tears sprang to her eyes. She promptly dashed them away with the back of her hand. "I'm sorry. I can't seem to stop crying."

"Yes, I know about Linus. I can only imagine the pain you're feeling right now. I'm really sorry, Stephanie. I know how much you cared about Linus. To tell you the truth, I'm missing the little guy pretty bad myself, too." He walked over to the window and placed the container of soup and the quilt on the table.

Questions swirled in Stephanie's head as she moved slowly toward him. "It's been awful, Acton. Just awful. Not just because I lost Linus, but…because I lost you."

His expression solemn, he shook his head. "I messaged you yesterday asking if we could talk. You never responded."

A few minutes after Faye Donovan had left the clinic, Stephanie had discovered Acton had sent a text message earlier that morning. Her first instinct had been to call him. But the timing had been all wrong.

She sighed. "I didn't respond because I…had to go home—to pack up all of Linus's things and get him ready to leave with his father. It wasn't a good time for us to talk."

Damn it. If only he'd known. He'd been a class A idiot. "I'm really sorry. I had no idea." He'd stop kicking himself eventually. Maybe in a year. "And now?" he asked gently.

Fearing another burst of tears was about to flood her eyes, she turned and walked over to the opposite side of the room. Standing near the fireplace, she stared out the window at the falling rain.

"We do have a lot to talk about," she said quietly.

At the sound of his footsteps, she glanced around to see him walking toward her and the look of yearning on his face caused her heart raced with anticipation and hope.

Stopping an arm's length away from her, he said, "And the first thing I need to say is that I'm sorry. Truly sorry."

Moisture filled her eyes as she met his gaze. "Oh, Acton, after we argued that day at Paws and Claws, and I'd had time to calm down and think more clearly I felt ashamed and guilty and stupid. Yes, I was knocked sideways over the news about Linus, but that was no excuse for shutting you out. And I'm sorry about that. You were right all along. Linus should be with his real father. That's the most important thing."

He moved a step closer and Stephanie was suddenly overwhelmed by his rugged face and familiar scent. She was going to have his baby and she wanted it, and him, more than she wanted anything in her life.

"You don't need to apologize to me, Stephanie. I

was the one who handled things badly. But that was because I wanted to be the one to comfort you—help you deal with losing Linus."

"I realize that now. But that day I wasn't thinking clearly, Acton. And then afterwards, when reality began to set in…well, I thought I'd blown everything between us." Her gaze somberly searched his face. "I think…the big problem is that I haven't been completely honest with you."

"You haven't? About what?"

"My feelings for you. I should have told you long before all of this happened with Linus that I love you. That I've been in love with you almost from the very start."

A mixture of amazement and doubt washed over his face. "Love? You love me? Why didn't you tell me?"

Her gaze dropped to the pearl snap in the middle of his chest. "Because a guy like you—you're not ready for marriage. And I was afraid it would make you run from me."

"Who says I'm not ready?"

She looked guiltily up at him. "Well, most everyone who knows you has told me that you—"

"That I'm a playboy?" he interrupted with a frown. "That I don't have a serious thought in my head? Well, they're wrong, Stephanie. Maybe on the outside that's what people think they see, but they don't know what's going on in here." He tapped the region of his heart. "I've been committed to our relationship from the very beginning, Stephanie. I love you, too, sweetheart. More than you'll ever know."

Hope bubbled inside her, but before she could truly let her heart celebrate, she had to tell him about the baby.

Biting down on her lip, she carefully studied his face. "You say that now, Acton, but you might feel differently when I tell you the rest."

Curious, he arched his eyebrows. "The rest? Your love comes with a condition?"

She smiled. Because when she thought about Acton's baby, that's the way it made her feel—happy. Oh, so happy.

"No. It comes with an addition. I'm pregnant, Acton. I'm going to have your baby."

His eyes grew wide. "Pregnant? You, me… We're going to have a baby?"

She nodded and, holding her breath, waited for his reaction.

It came with a smile that spread from ear to ear. "Oh, Stephanie! Wow! A baby for us! This is…amazing!"

"I realize it's unexpected and I haven't confirmed it with the doctor, but I've already taken a home-pregnancy test. And morning sickness is hitting me as soon as I lift my head off the pillow. I'm not sure how it happened exactly. But I think my pills are too weak, or you're too virile. Take your pick."

Suddenly he was laughing and hugging her tightly against him. "We're going to have a baby and you love me. The only way I could be any happier is if you agree to be by my side for the rest of our lives."

Leaning her head back, she smiled up at him. "Again, before I answer I have a condition."

"Okay, lay it on me. I'm guessing you're eventually going to want a giant wedding with twelve bridesmaids and me in a tuxedo."

She laughed. "The wedding doesn't have to be that big! As far as I'm concerned I'd be happy if we eloped to Las Vegas."

His blue eyes twinkled. "Hey, now that's a thought," he said, then asked, "So what is the condition?"

"That we make our home on the Diamond D— in your grandparents' farmhouse. Do you think you can make room for me, our baby and six more animals?"

Mystified, he gestured to their luxurious surroundings. "I can make room for all of you and more. But, Stephanie, what about this place? It's so grand and—"

"Yes, it's grand. But my home is with you—in the little house where we first made love. I want our children to be raised on the Diamond D, just like you." Her smile was full of love. "And don't worry about this place. My triplet sisters are planning to move to Rambling Rose soon to help with the restaurant. This part of the house will be perfect for them. And your house will be perfect for me. What do you think?"

"I came over here determined to fight for the woman I love. Now I'm thinking I'm the happiest man in the world." Dropping his head, he placed a long, sweet kiss on her lips. "I want us to get engaged soon, Stephanie. As soon as I can find the perfect ring. What do you say?"

"I say yes!"

Cradling her face in his hands, he rubbed his thumbs over her cheeks. "I do have one important question, though," he said. "Do you think Seymour and Grizabella will be willing to share their home with all your furry friends?"

Smiling cleverly, she brought her lips back to his. "Seymour and Grizabella will be glad to share. Remember, I can put special spells on animals."

Groaning, he pulled her tightly into his arms. "Mmm. And you've put one on me that's going to last a lifetime."

* * * * *

Look for the next installment of the new continuity
The Fortunes of Texas: Rambling Rose

Don't miss
The Mayor's Secret Fortune
by USA Today *bestselling author Judy Duarte*
On sale March 2020, wherever Harlequin books
and ebooks are sold.

And catch up with the previous
Fortunes of Texas titles:

Fortune's Fresh Start
by Michelle Major
Available now!

#2749 A PROMISE TO KEEP
Return to the Double C • by Allison Leigh

When Jed Dalloway started over, ranching a mountain plot for his recluse boss saved him. So when hometown girl April Reed offers a deal to develop the land, to protect his ailing mentor, Jed tells her no sale. But his heart doesn't get the message...

#2750 THE MAYOR'S SECRET FORTUNE
The Fortunes of Texas: Rambling Rose • by Judy Duarte

When Steven Fortune proposes to Ellie Hernandez, the mayor of Rambling Rose, no one is more surprised than Ellie herself. Until recently, Steven was practically her enemy! But his offer of a marriage of convenience arrives at her weakest moment. Can they pull off a united front?

#2751 THE BEST INTENTIONS
Welcome to Starlight • by Michelle Major

A string of bad choices led Kaitlin Carmody to a fresh start in a small town. But Finn Samuelson, her boss's stubborn son, is certain she is taking advantage of his father and ruining his family's bank. When attraction interferes, Finn must decide if Kaitlin is really a threat to his family or its salvation.

#2752 THE MARRIAGE RESCUE
The Stone Gap Inn • by Shirley Jump

When a lost pup reunites Grady Jackson with his high school crush, he doesn't expect to become engaged! Marriage wasn't in dog groomer Beth Cooper's immediate plans, either. But if showing off her brand-new fiancé makes her dying father happy, how can she say, "I don't"?

#2753 A BABY AFFAIR
The Parent Portal • by Tara Taylor Quinn

Amelia Grace has gone through hell, but she's finally ready to be a mom—all by herself. Still, she never expected her sperm donor to appear, let alone spark an attraction like Dr. Craig Harmon does. But can Amelia make room for another person in her already growing family?

#2754 THE RIGHT MOMENT
Wildfire Ridge • by Heatherly Bell

After Joanne Brant is left at the altar, Hudson Decker must convince his best friend that Mr. Right is standing right in front of her! He missed his chance back in the day, but Hudson is sure now is the right moment for their second chance. Except Joanne's done giving people the chance to break her heart.

YOU CAN FIND MORE INFORMATION ON UPCOMING HARLEQUIN TITLES, FREE EXCERPTS AND MORE AT HARLEQUIN.COM.

HSECNM0220

SPECIAL EXCERPT FROM

◆ HARLEQUIN
SPECIAL EDITION

*When Jed Dalloway started over, ranching a
mountain plot for his recluse boss is what saved him.
So when hometown girl April Reed offers a deal
to develop the land, Jed tells her no sale.
But his heart doesn't get the message...*

*Read on for a sneak preview of
the next book in* New York Times *bestselling author
Allison Leigh's Return to the Double C miniseries,*
A Promise to Keep.

"Don't look at me like that, April."

She raised her gaze to his. "Like what?"

His fingers tightened in her hair and her mouth ran dry.
She swallowed. Moistened her lips.

She wasn't sure if she moved first. Or if it was him.

But then his mouth was on hers and like everything
else about him, she felt engulfed by an inferno. Or maybe
the burning was coming from inside her.

There was no way to know.

No reason to care.

Her hands slid up the granite chest, behind his neck,
where his skin felt even hotter beneath her fingertips, and
slipped through his thick hair, which was not hot, but
instead felt cool and unexpectedly silky.

His arm around her tightened, his hand pressing her
closer while his kiss deepened. Consuming. Exhilarating.

Her head was whirling, sounds roaring.

It was only a kiss.

But she was melting.

She was flying.

And then she realized the sounds weren't just inside her head.

Someone was laying on a horn.

She jerked back, her gaze skittering over Jed's as they both turned to peer through the curtain of white light shining over them.

"Mind getting at least one of these vehicles out of the way?" The shout was male and obviously amused.

"Oh for cryin'—" She exhaled. "That's my uncle Matthew," she told Jed, pushing him away. "And I'm sorry to say, but we are probably never going to live this down."

Don't miss
A Promise to Keep *by Allison Leigh,*
available March 2020 wherever
Harlequin Special Edition books and ebooks are sold.

Harlequin.com

HSEEXP0220

Love Harlequin romance?

DISCOVER.
Be the first to find out about promotions, news and exclusive content!

 Facebook.com/HarlequinBooks

Twitter.com/HarlequinBooks

 Instagram.com/HarlequinBooks

Pinterest.com/HarlequinBooks

ReaderService.com

EXPLORE.
Sign up for the Harlequin e-newsletter and download a free book from any series at
TryHarlequin.com

CONNECT.
Join our Harlequin community to share your thoughts and connect with other romance readers!
Facebook.com/groups/HarlequinConnection

HSOCIAL2020